FREI

A   TALES

FREUD IN CONEY ISLAND
AND OTHER TALES

Norman M. Klein

To Jean,

[After] her
endless journey
across the world!
So pleased to meet
at last.

Very Best,

OTIS BOOKS/SEISMICITY EDITIONS

The Graduate Writing Program
Otis College of Art and Design

BEALL CENTER FOR ART AND TECHNOLOGY

University of California, Irvine
LOS ANGELES ● 2006

Book design and typesetting: Yuko Sawamoto

BEALL CENTER FOR ART AND TECHNOLOGY
University of California, Irvine

OTIS BOOKS/SEISMICITY EDITIONS
The Graduate Writing Program
Otis College of Art and Design
9045 Lincoln Boulevard
Los Angeles, CA 90045

www.otis.edu
seismicity@otis.edu

An admirer of Freud sent him the following in 1938, unsigned—and also unopened for some reason. It was recovered among Freud's papers. Here is a key paragraph:

"There is nothing more unreliable than the plain facts. They always make me ask: What exactly did not get included? Or who decides what to leave out? Most of all, do these facts work like my memory? I always forget where I put things."

It has taken us ten years to discover the poor soul who wrote this, but more importantly, what her letter implies about mass entertainment since 1909; and the psychological impact of special effects. Her puzzle began with a very plain fact in Freud's life, but it was even more clearly about the comic pleasures of the grotesque.

With that said, let me rush into the first tale, before I change my mind.

The facts are simple enough: In September, 1909, a relatively unknown Freud spent a week in New York City, en route to a lecture series upstate at Clark University. The air ranged from muggy to stifling. The museum exhibition on antiquities, the one he had high hopes for, proved substandard. The crowds on the street smelled of industrial fluids and sweat. Even friendly faces made him squirm. The conductor on a tram tried to be empathetic: he ordered the crowd to make room for "the old man." But Freud did not see himself as old, not yet. He pulled back his shoulders and glared, then felt idiotic.

Back in the hotel, his stomach was churning from American food. His mouth tasted like rancid milk. His neck felt numb. I'm truly a mass of symptoms, he told himself. I'm a neurasthenic woman. I'll wake up paralyzed on my left side. I need a day by the sea. He rummaged through his trunk for a lighter suit. In the morning, before the sewer vapors hit the sidewalks once again, he took a ferry to Coney Island. Of course increasingly, as we know now, he kept these anxieties–his own case study–in separate leather notebooks, a psychiatric form of double book-keeping...

As the boat chugged along, smoke from Manhattan evaporated into blue mist. Finally, the ferry anchored at Dreamland Pier (what someone called Old Iron Pier). A friendly gust of sea air greeted him, but the view made him wince, like architectural gastritis. A lunatic tower dominated, built like a hodge-podge–vaguely Moorish on top, wedding-cake Venetian in the middle, a wigwam at the bottom. Clustered around it were buildings so tentative, so flimsy, they could have been built with egg shells; they were sketches in pasteboard. Then, toward the horizon, he saw streets that looked like the day after mardi gras, like a gigantic drunken operetta.

Luckily it was still early in the morning. Even the mist had not burned off yet. The main streets, Surf Avenue and the Bowery, looked sleepy. But then the turmoil began. Within an hour, they were already jammed with confusion. Armies seemed to be scattering in retreat. Freud tried to hide on the beach, but after a few hours, decided to enter the "irresponsible gaiety." He started taking notes in one of those leather journals that would remain hidden, even from many friends and admirers, for ninety years.

At the entrance to Luna Park, he noticed two monkeys on a chain, mother and child. The mother was baring her teeth and hissing, while a crowd poked at her little boy, some with umbrellas, canes, some with their index fingers. The monkey child's movements utterly reminded him of children he had treated, a monkey Little Hans. If this were an infant, a shock this fierce would undoubtedly lead to phobic behavior. What if monkeys stored this shock in an early mental place, a primal sod? And what if this atavistic place survived, while the species evolved–like gills or tail bones inside the fetus? It would lie hidden below more intricate formations. And yet, it would still operate as a mechanism, perhaps fainter in humans than monkeys; or even more convoluted, like folds on the brain. Surely there would be no therapeutic way to find a psychic spot so ancient.

The monkey child under attack stared agonistically, almost christlike. Freud tried to interpret its sublunar gaze, but its eyes were a deep onyx. He managed to capture this thought in only a single sentence, beneath complaints about the boiled sausage he had just eaten.

There is reason to believe that Freud walked into Dreamland, the last and most bourgeois of the three amusement parks in Coney Island. To enter, one had to pass through "Creation," a music-hall version of Genesis. Creation began at the mouth of a huge tunnel, featuring the massive thighs and vagina of a plaster nude thirty feet high. Her breasts were larger than haystacks. She sparked at least two sentences. A phrase from one survives, in the recently uncovered *Freud Ephemera*: "... or do Americans prefer genitalia large enough to crush a man, or at least ruin his hat?" As many scholars have noted since the *Freud Ephemera* turned up in London (1999), biblical fantasy was highly eroticized in Coney Island, or turned into a circus freak show, with little boys as mephistopheles selling bags of peanuts, and dwarves with their own freak town.

We are also reasonably certain that Freud went to Hell, not only the Hell Gate in Dreamland; but also Darkness and Dawn (with Hell as Darkness) in Luna Park. He enjoyed watching the Chicago Fire (with women jumping from flaming windows). Nearby, he claimed his hair was nearly singed when the riverboat Prairie Belle burst into flames along the Mississippi. He even yawned his way down "Stygian chambers," to the River Styx; and saw the Flood at the Crack of Dawn.

Hell Gate at Dreamland caught his attention most of all, particularly its shoddy construction, and miserable ventilation. The fires of the damned were made of crepe paper. The walls of Hell were papier maché. A reasonable Flood from God could have dissolved it all in five minutes. But the mood in Hell had a "strangeness and irresponsible gaiety" that Freud assumed was an American problem. Americans like cheerful torture, he decided. Fairy-tale rape Jung would probably call it (Jung would have a field day with all this). "Americans will take a long trolley ride just to pretend to be buried alive. They think being molested by circus freaks is the most uncanny (*unheimlich*) thing of all."

A pretty red-haired girl caught Freud's eye, as she wandered into Hell Gate. A girl of twenty, she adjusted her new bonnet, posed cheerfully in the mirror. Suddenly, demons in cheap tights grabbed her. With a look of supreme boredom, they lifted her by her armpits. The more she kicked and cursed, the harder they laughed. Then they dumped her like a dead cat down a long trough. Her taffeta undergarment rustled while she skidded out of sight. Afterward, the demons turned and cackled mindlessly for the crowd. An exhausted, obviously gin-soaked Satan snickered his approval. This stale laughter was supposed to be infectious.

Meanwhile, the young lady's screams faded away. In like manner, her sliding body seemed to hit bottom. Freud heard a faint thud. But then two minutes later, she came storming back. Angrily, she planted her new hat (a tuque or toque) back on her head. Then she gestured rudely, "in a masculine way," at the demons and Satan. Puffing up, she looked ready to slap someone, but then, inexplicably did not. Instead she broke into a smile. After all, Freud wrote, she had just paid at least ten cents to be there. Within twenty minutes, eleven more well-dressed women were thrown down one hole or another; with barely a peep from any of them, like dover soles being dressed and boned. But that was not the only indignity women had to suffer "with a smile." At the Luna Park next door, many well appointed ladies, even ladies of a certain age, were shoved on top of a small hole where a large gust of air blew their dress above their thigh. Then everyone was supposed to whoop it up. Thank goodness my wife and daughter are back in Vienna, Freud noted. Imagine them disappearing like shit down a hole, with their thighs exposed. A newspaper he found called this "a nightmare world that claims to be bizarre and fantastic."

In German, Freud detailed a sermon given at Hell Gate, to justify everything he had seen. A wholesome preacher approached like a sturdy tenor ("the face of a farmer, the look of a swindler"). Men should not squeeze unmarried women, the preacher declared. Nor should women "outcasts" steal from drunken men. In fact, all whiskey and beer "arouses the passions." But most of all, one must keep Satan from your door: be sure to pay your preachers as much as you can afford. Then, Freud heard the ceiling begin to ache. He looked up. It was barely supporting a fat archangel sliding on a wire. Satan gasped loudly, then went into bad pantomime. He howled like a man screaming on cue, then dived down a pit.

Afterward, Freud lingered in Hell for at least twenty minutes more. Then two demons came by. They warned him to stop writing, then began to cackle, and head in his direction. So he left in a hurry. But there lies the scholarly problem: how did Freud understand the sermon in English? Clearly by then he had been joined by a friend of Sàndor Ferenczi, probably two friends. It appears that Ferenczi was too busy setting up the lecture series, so he sent these two unlikely people in his stead. They were his former patients, "success stories that proved the genius of psychoanalysis." What's more, they knew Coney Island all too well, and spoke German and Yiddish. First there was a pretty woman in her early thirties, with a full face and large brooding eyes. Like a parody of a therapist, she tended to her high-strung cousin, a man with the same deeply sunken eyes, and a peculiar scar from his earlobe down to his jaw.

Guiding Freud back to Surf Avenue, they paid ten cents to have his picture taken (not the faked photograph so often assumed to be Freud, but the photo in Folio 7 of the *Ephemera*). Here we see Freud in a cloud of confusion, fighting for his dignity. We literally see him looking up with suspicion. He was getting hints of what he was up against. Then the facts were made plain: The man, named Al, was haunted by the unspent yearnings of a dead relative. He felt "her" crawling inside his chest, whispering to him. Over the years, she had "forced" him into horrible business investments that wasted the family fortune. She (or it) had also coaxed Al into chilly love affairs with dull women that she found acceptable. But to Al, they were invariably too scrawny, too squinty, too withdrawn.

However lately, Al had stopped feeling haunted. Thanks to Frida, he was now applying Ferenczi's collective hypnosis to silence the dead relative. By contrast, only three months ago, this dead voice—whose name could not be spoken out loud, not even written down—had forced Al to hear the pumping of blood throughout his body. "Dead Relative" (as he called her) had sensed a constriction somewhere. She warned Al that he was due for a massive heart attack. Al fell into a panic. He listened sleeplessly to the burbling of his arteries, until at last, he went into false angina, and found himself in the hospital.

But nothing like that invaded this cheerful late afternoon (not yet). Al was doing "fine, feeling chipper." With Al doing so well, Freud shifted his attention elsewhere. He noticed that Frida had immensely long eyelashes. Surely behind those yes, she had serious reaction formations as well, he thought. Why else would she devote herself like a sister of mercy to Al? He clearly was not available, not for romance, not even for much conversation—"not this year," she said, rather pointedly.

The two cousins (or was that three, with Dead Relative in hiding?) ushered Freud to a bath house near Steeplechase Park. They translated for Freud in English. His throat was parched. They got him a frozen ice. Then with a loud sigh, Freud plumped on to a rented steam chair, and nodded off instantly. However, as Folio 7.6 indicates, he then slipped into rather frantic dreams. At the height of his busy sleep, he saw Frida staring at him. Her immense eyes were floating or ticking like a clock. Her stare awoke him with a start. He sat bolt upright, in a sweat. There indeed was Frida looming over him. She had been studying him and gathering her thoughts.

Through Ferenczi, (his reverent disciple, at least in 1909), she had been absorbing Freud's newest book about Little Hans, the five-year old phobic boy; and also the recent case study of the Rat Man, about *zwangsneurose*, obsessive-compulsive neurosis. (She was only beginning to internalize his Wolf Man essay.) And now, as if by miracle, less than a week after she had returned home, the author himself was having troubled dreams before her, twisting and turning right there in the flesh. It was only weeks since her self-hypnosis with Ferenczi (and Al) had undergone that famous breakthrough (cited in Gottlieb, et al.). There Freud was, supine, still dapper at 53, hair only faintly gray, though a little matted from all he had been through. Just seeing him sparked insights. But she had learned through bitter experience that when you speak to bright men, frame your words very slowly, and tilt your head toward the light. We only have the gist of what she said, though it went on for some time. First she posed a question (while posing, so to speak):

"Suppose reaction formations are driven by erotic denial?"

Freud answered: "Yes, they are."

"Well then," she went on, "can reaction formations act on groups? That is, the same as it affects people alone?"

"Perhaps," Freud answered, then thought again.

"Yes, of course... It must."

"Well (stretching her neck for a moment, pausing to catch the light)... that means a group plays by the same emotional rules as a person alone. Basically?"

The late afternoon cast a spell over her face. She smiled and reworded her question: "Put it another way. Let's take the crowd at Hell Gate. Does their phobic play work the same as Little Hans by himself?"

Freud stared at her with renewed interest. Sensing his approval, she ranted on about Coney Island attractions for ten minutes or more. Freud particularly remembered her description of men who loved being zapped by electrical prods in Luna Park. Then he noticed that her palm was moist when she squeezed his hand. Her eyes transformed from hazel to coral in the late afternoon light. But even worse, her mouth reminded him of Sabina Spielrein, the patient with the sway in her walk. Freud knew that she was already Jung's mistress. Jung, that *kuppler* (pimp), had even coaxed her to write to Freud, asking him to mop up the affair. Jung sent her to Freud like a taste of meat left on the bone, to show off the line of her face, the slim neck.

The sun burned into the ocean, leaving Frida in silhouette. Freud shifted his head, and like an optical illusion, Sabina's face substituted for Frida.

As Freudian scholars know, this was not the first time that he underwent this phenomenon, simply the most haunting, the most cited in the *Ephemera*. Facial transpositions often bothered Freud. Usually, they came during the third or fourth year of extensive therapy. Frida had simply jumped a few steps ahead. Freud often compared these transpositions to phosphenes caused by the sun. "A husband transposes his mother's face on to his wife's naked body," he wrote in 1916, then crossed it out.

As R.R. Greenblatt pointed out, at the groundbreaking conference on the *Ephemera* (2002), "Freud tried to live above or below the erotic fixations that he discussed." Frida's answer was even simpler. To her, Coney Island was a psychiatric teeter-totter. Reality keeps uneasy company with pleasure, she said. The outside pretends to have collective sex with the inside.

Freud answered with a sociological theory. "The lower classes in Coney Island are not as sexually repressed as the cultured classes," he declared, his voice rising. Case closed. He slammed his notebook, to emphasize, punctuate–when something from outside floated toward him. He sensed a ripple of hysteria fifty yards away. Al was spinning like a dervish, his arms splayed outward as he turned. A crowd of beer drinkers formed a circle to watch. Al became an attraction. He had just seen a dwarf on Surf Avenue who completely, I mean utterly resembled the Dead Relative. Suddenly, the weather turned gloomy around him. Voices came at him. Four of these voices felt like winds landing on his head, making the shape of a cross. Next, Al heard music that sounded like insects climbing into his ears, making him dizzy with vertigo. Frida was heart-struck. Freud had to serve as the doctor in the house. Two hours passed (no notes). But clearly the day went from bad to much worse.

Some time after eight, Jung may have arrived, and Ferenczi they say. That is, of course, what biographies have told us, that they cruised and schmoozed together, a genteel evening by the sea. But now we know that Freud asked his friends, particularly Jung and Ferenczi, to hide events of his day in Coney Island. I am not convinced why. It was not simply those two patients. Al's episode, his catalytic ferment, as Ferenczi called it, should not have overwhelmed Freud. No doubt, something larger convinced everyone to maintain silence for the rest of their lives. Even Ernest Jones was kept out of the loop.

Now however, the *Ephemera* restores part of that day, though not enough. We are still left to fill in the blanks. At least two hours are missing, perhaps even twelve, from morning through night. Frida brought Freud back to his hotel. Something may have happened that night or the next day. Five years later, Frida married a career officer in the German army, but by 1920, she had disappeared. Al meanwhile slogged along for decades, lived an astonishing long life on vapors, like bacteria living on a rock.

He died as haunted as ever, but with a heart going as strong as a furnace, at the ripe age of seventy-four. His brain simply gave way, but he never had a cold in his life. Paranoia kept him fresh.

Now we return to that week in New York. Standard documents leave us only a few dyspeptic facts: Soon after visiting Coney Island, both Freud and Jung suffered diarrhea, each on different days. New York food troubled them. That is well established. Also, on the Wednesday after Coney Island, Freud went to Columbia University, where he involuntarily urinated down his pants, left a mortally embarrassing stain. He and Jung discussed whether he should enter therapy for the problem. And some time that year, once if not twice, he and Jung plunged into one of their fiercest oedipal arguments, partially only about Sabina, mostly about the paranormal. As their rage steamed the wallpaper off the walls, Freud simply fainted; he hyperventilated, or fell very briefly into grief at the loss of his "adoptive" son. No wonder he called America a land of savages.

By 1914, Sabina was replaced by Toni Wolff as Jung's mistress, as a permanent "aunt" for his children. Jung, in turn, hinted that Freud had sex with Sabina. Freud exploded. That was the end of their dysfunctional family. Now the *Ephemera* answers some of the nagging questions about Ferenczi's private adventures as well.

Right before transmogrifying in front of Freud that day, Frida had gone back to Hungary for six months to be treated by Ferenczi. There she met a married man of limited potential named Moscowitz, who changed his name to Klein in order to dance as a gentile in the Austrian Empire—mostly to get away from his wife, the farm, the goats, the grist mill, the cheese. "M+K," as Ferenczi calls him in his notes, had a step sister in Budapest who was something of a panderer. She ran a rooming house in Budapest that often rented to women of an "uncertain reputation." Ferenczi warned Frida against staying there, but Al seemed to be less haunted around prostitutes. That made the day, at least, much easier for Frida. So she left Al there, while she stayed with

M+K. But every night, she returned to the rooming house, to drag Al back to earth, and take him to the music hall. There M+K performed what one reviewer called the worst dance act in Budapest. But M+K was indefatigably cheerful, a relief from Al. That allowed Frida to be loyal to all the men in her life. After the show, she could walk Al back to the rooming house. There Al met his favorite, a young Polish girl whose pubic hair was very red, like a fox in a burrow he used to say. Afterward, Frida pretended to sway in rhythm to M+K flying high beside her, reenacting his czárdas as they wandered home.

Finally, after a few months, M+K took a train back to his village, near what is now the Slovakian border. His son's wife was about to give birth to his grandson, who would be known as Young Yussell, a Yiddish nickname for the Hebrew name for Jesus. But Young Yussell was hardly a Jesus, certainly not a mystic, even when ghosts crossed his path. For example, when he was ten, in the chaos after the Great War, Young Yussell finished tending the goats as the sun went down, and walked to a clearing in the woods near the farm. There he saw an old table thirty feet long. The surface had been carved with an adze hundreds of years ago. The table was piled with roasted meats. Dozens of revelers were eating loudly. They were dressed in what Yussell called "very old clothing." When asked what he meant, he answered, "older than anyone wears anymore." They wore tights and codpieces. Some had feathered hats. The leather of their shoes and shirts was tanned in the old way. They were from another century.

He walked up to the table, and it disappeared. With the table gone, he could see the clearing through the moonlight back to the farm. Yussell never wondered what had taken place. Why question, he asked? Did the ghosts leave any food for me? Yussell believed the earth was no rounder than you could walk in a day. It was flat because your shoes were flat. It was no more haunted than bugs on your food, or a smell where you sat.

But through Frida, Yussell's ghost story finally came to Ferenczi's attention. He used it as ammunition against Freud's argument about the insoluble nature of the unconscious. Freud answered in this way:

> A man who feels a great thirst at night after enjoying highly seasoned food for supper, often dreams that he is drinking. Of course, the dream never satisfies a strong desire for food or drink. Young Yussell had probably missed supper. But even as a boy, he knew that you cannot quench your thirst by dreaming. From such a dream, one awakes thirsty, and the hallucination dries up in the moonlight. That is your folklore for you, your haunted forest.

For example, in 1913, Freud complained of patients who dreamt in fairy tales, conjuring up Rumpilstiltskin, and so on. He decided that they were satisfying a wish fulfillment, but not out of collective folk memory. Instead, they were dreaming of moments from their childhood nursery (screen memory). A patient dreams of a copy of Doré's illustrations to *Perrault's Tales* (1867). One image haunts him, is engrammed in his memory, of Little Red Riding Hood lying in bed beside the wolf. She stares ahead in dreamy anticipation. The Wolf's great snout is almost handsome, very carefully modeled. In the end, it remained clear to Freud that neither folk tales nor popular illustrations nor Coney Island—nor a visit to the Acropolis or the Loch Ness monster—could generate dream work, not in the way that the Id (the primal I) did.

Something like narcissism, depersonalization or infantile regression might generate Yussell's brief identity crisis. These were hallucinatory flashes, again like Freud at the Acropolis, but nothing on the order of what we find in Freud's notebooks about Coney Island (discussed variously in Folios 7–9). When the codex of the *Ephemera* finally appears (2007), the public will see what a few scholars have confronted since its discovery in 1999. Readers will have to take the same journey. It turns out that his day in Coney Island extends for another eighty years at least. It echoes throughout the twentieth century, easily from 1909 to 1989, even to 2004.

We return to that day for more clues. In 1918, he writes:

> From the boardwalk, I saw women in bustles and women in stone, but not stone. It was a warm day, as warm as the Prater on a Sunday in summer. I remember New York from the boardwalk, and have hidden what it suggested about some of my work. I do not suppose anyone will need to know about my casual impressions of Coney Island in 1908.

We know, of course, that the boardwalk was not formally installed in Coney Island until 1920, not all seven miles from the parks to Sea Gate. Only the Bowery remained as part of an earlier boardwalk. Freud even mistakenly dates his visit to "the American Prater" as 1908, as if the crises with Jung in 1909 had not happened yet. But most of all, clearly the elegance of the Prater was hardly the same as the roaring half-mile of the Bowery boardwalk. Consider this description in 1908:

> Busy blocks–eating booths, hot frankfurters on the grill, beef dripping on the spit, wash-boilers of green corn steaming in the center of hungry groups who gnawed on (them) as if playing harmonicas; photograph galleries, the sitters ghastly in the charnel-house glare... open-faced moving picture shows (that) invite effrontery from the jocose crowd; chop suey joints, fez-topped palmists, strength tests; dance halls and continuous song-and-dance entertainments; girls... in tights and spangles (except on the Sabbath). Bands, orchestras, pianos at war with gramophones, hand-organs, calliopes; overhead, a roar of wheels in a death lock with shrieks and screams; whistles, gongs, rifles all busy; the smell of candy, popcorn, meats, beer, tobacco, blended with the odor of the crowd redolent now and then of patchouli; a steaming river of people, arches over by electric signs–this is the Bowery at Coney Island.

We also know that Freud saw his first moving pictures that week, possibly at Coney Island; and was again singularly unimpressed, like the classic statement by Kafka a few years later, that movies were only "iron shutters" that disturb one's vision, forcing the eye to jump from one vision to another, 'putting the eye into uniform." (We know, of course, that Freud always compared his day in Coney Island to the hounds of world war). It was indeed so difficult for turn-of-the-century modernists (Freud, Kafka, Bergson) who were shaped before mass entertainment took charge, to perceive its imagery as more than the sweat of the crowd.

Anyway, by 1928, Freud had completed his meta-theory about Coney Island as a "sidelong glance," in notes about group dynamics, transference neurosis, the psychopathology of everyday life, lay analysis, taboo systems. But the crisis was not laid to rest, not even as displacement, particularly after the war. Freud even mentally returned to Coney Island (Folio 9) as he labored over his answer to Rousseau, *Civilization and Its Discontents*. But even there, the phobic play of the crowds in Coney Island had to remain scrupulously outside of his system. "I have invented a map like a wall brick by brick," he writes. "But the exception makes the map," he added. Thus, in the *Ephemera*, the Coney Island material defines what he calls *abseits liegend*, "outlying." It was basic to the place that could not be mapped into his topology, even at the end of his life, particularly by the end (as in references to the hounds of war as a thrill ride). We see Freud dying of cancer of the jaw on the eve of the Second World War. One of his final notes refers to a dark Coney-Island like hallucination. As the pain and the opium ripen together, he describes "the spiral dream," where "phobic play" converts into spiraling machines crushing his Europe.

Of course, 1928 became another milestone, we now know. However, why a milestone still remains unclear. We are forced one more time into guess work. What was so riveting to Freud about this particular "surprise" in 1928? That is, after so many other surprises appear as cryptographic references in the *Ephemera*, what Greenblatt calls "his secret language to himself as a twin." All we know is that, for perhaps the twentieth time from 1905 to 1928, Freud withheld what he called a "surprise." He isolated it from his public record. Even in Folio 9, he reveals only enough for him to remember. As he wrote in the *Addendum*: "To know that you will be plundered (*da wirst geplundert*) like a ruin for a thousand years is to be haunted by the future." At any rate, this "surprise" of 1928 (he called it *uberraselung,* an oddly antique word) apparently required special handling. It was a last straw of some kind, an event he kept from his family as well. Freud had to change the diaries as a result, make a structural revision. In the summer of 1928, he gathered the leather Folios 7–9, then added 1–8; and converted them into a secret incunabula, of sorts. Each volume was fitted in its box (so often compared to a cigar box). And within each box, he also inserted the famous "lost" photos, sketches and other ephemera (thus the name). All nine boxes were then joined like a piece of crude marquetry inside a larger case, something built for him that could be locked up.

This case traveled with Freud when he left his apartment for London in 1937. He described it once as "the relic of a family pet." For the crossing to London, it was wrapped in a blanket, and stored inside a steamer trunk. A year later, as his illness worsened, he planned for the future of his incunabula. He set up the unknown last requests. And they were observed to the letter, as far as we know. Finally, even the requests themselves were permanently lost, when the family servant entrusted with them died in 1954. Not until 1999 did the waterlogged wooden crate finally turn up. At first, it was catalogued, and auctioned off, as "a handmade typewriter case filled with travel diaries by an Austrian physician, circa 1920."

But let us return to another key event from 1928: Freud's meetings with Soviet artist/designer El Lissitzky. They already knew each other, perhaps as early as 1922, but only casually. In the Fall of 1928, however, they met for days. We imagine the two international Jews struggling over a coffee at first, trying to find a common interest, a common humanity. They politely disagree about America, about its potential. Freud drops hints about strange notes on America (*fremdheit*), private scribblings, not a part of his public lectures.

"I have often wondered," Freud said," if the shape of Coney Island parks resembles my model of the mind. By that I mean, does real space reproduce unconscious space?"

Lissitzky, the former architect, the constructivist spatial designer (PROUNs) was thrilled by the concept. Was there a way, beyond the ghoulish cuteness of amusement parks, to build a space where the symptoms and formations of Freud's theories could be acted out–to walk around Freud's model as if at a theater or in a cathedral, or on a city boulevard?

Freud and Lissitzky began to imagine what shape this phantasmagoria should assume (*Trugbild, Wahngebilde*). Freud's version suggested an inveterate Viennese on a long walk inside the Ring. He kept returning to the layer-cake design of Viennese housing, with its half floor above the store level–that would be a preconscious–followed by cathectic, aseptic layers above. The boiler in the basement he saw as a kind of *Ich* or Id. It radiated heat like "vengeance rising through the floorboards." A roof leaking cathected from overhead, also like the Id: "to be invaded by pent-up weather is a dream of drowning in your parent's embrace."

Lissitzky preferred something more functional, yet whimsical, like his Lenin's lecture tower, a much more open floor plan for the unconscious. Instead of Freud's sketch of the unconscious in only two tiers above ground (one for childhood shock, one for adult neurosis), Lissitzky needed something more imbricated. One day, he brought Sabbattini's old manual from 1638, about how to build illusions in the theater, for example, how to turn a man into a stone and back again.

Inside Sabbatini, he found evidence explaining Freud's quote about the Prater. When it came to architecture, Freud preferred a soothing unconscious, where humans and motorized statues from their life (like an amusement park) cohabitated in Baroque elegance, like Descartes' fascination with automatons designed as a singing lake. But Lissitzky's maquette included motorized walls and ceilings as well, an "ideogrammatic machine." His "cine-collage" model even influenced Eisenstein for a few months (generating a brief film by Eisenstein, now lost–about two minutes long). But Lissitzky's package never returned to the Soviet Union. With the coming of the first five-year plan, and with the momentous suicide of Mayakovsky, Lissitzky decided to leave his *Freud/PROUN* in Germany. He built a small, motorized journey zigzagging on an hydraulic stage, filled with electromagnetic puppets, and sliding involutions, like cilia or a Coney-Island mystery ride, to reenact cathexis in a Freudian space; along with vectors of water forming psycho-ideograms on sheets of glass against one wall, that was also incised with names that Freud wrote especially for the project, including Dreamland and Hell Gate.

Lissitzky's design, with Freud's commentary, were stored in a basement in Bremen. There they hibernated until 1966, when the architect Sándor Hartobagi found them. Behind a sketch on wood, Hartobagi peeled away three pages, sticky from moisture, and a rusty, warped model. Most of the text had been eaten away by fungus, like a dead sea scroll. A signature indicated someone called "Ds. Df ." Even Hartobagi guessed that it was an inversion of s..igmund f...reud. However, not until 1999 was the handwriting verified as Freud; along with more on *Freud/PROUN* found in Folio 9 of the *Ephemera*.

Why so long for this discovery to emerge? Hartobagi's brief essay, with architectural charts, came out only in Hungarian, so *Freud/PROUN* disappeared once again (in a language not widely read). However, it survived as urban legend for young architects in pre-war Vienna, particularly for Victor Gruen. Finally, after the shocks of the war, in 1956, the émigré Gruen made his mark in the US. He completed the first of his many multi-level enclosed malls, the Southdale Shopping Center in the Edina suburb of Minneapolis. At the historic opening, after three vodka martinis and no sleep for two days, Gruen made a slip of the tongue, a parapraxis. Freud ephemerist, Ute Margaret Flynn explains: "Flushed with excitement, perhaps a little drunk, Gruen promised a future dominated by Viennese shopping agoras, PROUNs he called them. He felt himself retracing the steps of Dr. Freud inside the Ringstrasse, 'into an American Prater, a shopper's Coney Island.'"

In 1986, the Hungarian computer designer, Zsolt Bohus spotted the article. He became obsessed with developing it into a computer game, for American providers outsourcing to Hungary. The Bohus game design, with steam and prairie fires and nightmare rides, with the super ego spitting venom and the preconscious boiling and spewing, went out for review–to test its commercial potential. It finally passed to Fred Blazs, an executive at an American game company (name withheld); also married to a psychiatrist (thus, he seemed the logical choice). However, Blazs explained that first of all, he had just been divorced; and secondly, in court, his wife complained publicly that he had no unconscious at all. And on top of all that: what is the reward system for psychotherapy? "Remember these are kids passing puberty, in their underwear, playing computer games at two in the morning." Blazs was famous in the industry for saying: "In the next hundred years, we all will pass puberty over and over again, in game after game." That certainly would not qualify him as Freudian.

This Freud game (simply called *Id*) does not get past the radar at Disney's Epcot Center either. Besides, why would Disney want visitors to discover their own unconscious? Indeed, Frida's warnings had come to roost. Mass culture was now shaping unconscious drives en masse, warp drives. It was building user-friendly wish fulfillment–ergonomically scripted spaces, what Klein calls consumer Calvinism: the myth of free will in a world of absolute predestination. We no longer can easily separate the latent from the manifest. As an editorial in a recent advertising journal explains; "Consumers don't need an unconscious, only better medication. An unexamined life shops."

As for Young Yussell–our only link to Frida and M+K–he winds up in America, first in Pittsburgh, brought there by his father, a pesky old man with a taste for bad advice and schnapps. When Yussell was twelve, and still herding goats in Hungary, his father wrote: "Yussell, some day I will bring the entire family here to Pittsburgh. But you as the oldest son must get ready. Only one skill can save you in America. Learn this one thing, and you will be a success. Learn to play the violin."

So Yussel spent the next eight years sawing away at a cheap violin, then through his aunt, the rooming-house owner in Budapest, he got a slightly better tuned, perhaps stolen violin, as a birthday present.

But imagine how useless playing the violin was when Yussell arrived in 1928. By the time he learned English, Pittsburgh was sinking into the Great Depression. Yussell eventually used his fine motor skills to become a kosher butcher.

His father, the boozy son of M+K, had other plans altogether. He decided to retire the moment that his sons arrived in Pittsburgh, and refine his love of schnapps and other sweet whiskies (Southern Comfort, single malt scotch whiskies, Glenfarclas when he could afford a pint). Finally, the family moved to Brooklyn, where he became a rag man, wheeling his little wagon behind movie theaters to watch an afternoon double bill. Then after *ma'arev* (evening prayer, with honey cake and schnapps), he would return home exhausted from the long day, itching for another pick me up.

Yussell married, though not happily. He fathered two children, who spent most of their formative years wishing they were somewhere else. Finally, Yussell brought them to Coney Island, as if following a voice from a dead relative–an insistent woman's voice that came to him in a haze, and usually filled him with bad advice. But at least she just whispers, he reasoned. Taking advice from this voice, Yussell developed an unerring instinct for moving to neighborhoods just as they start to decline. Coney Island began to sink like a stone almost the day after he arrived, or at least within the year.

His son, Norman (often confused with the author of this piece) was an anxious, fretful child, afraid of his own shadow, also afflicted, in Yussell's words, with "no common sense." What's more, Norman began to have strange nightmares after they moved to Coney Island, particularly about a woman with large glowing eyes, like a mole. Luckily, Norman never remembers his dreams.

But something obviously lingered, like sour breath after a heavy meal. In 1995, while teaching media classes to computer animators, Norman became obsessed with Freud in Coney Island. As if by intuition, he began imagining a game he called Sim-Freud.

By 1998, this game settled in his mind like a pigeon on a ledge. One night, while he slept, a particle from a down pillow went into his ear. It imbalanced his canals. He woke up with benign positional vertigo. Suddenly, he couldn't distinguish front from back. The wind blowing on his face felt like a blast of air behind him. When he walked, the floor rose like liquid, rinsing and churning. But gradually, his brain made adjustments. It did not repair the imbalance, simply adjusted to it. His brain told his eyes to stop feeling nauseous or dizzy. That made upside-down appear right-side up. It adjusted his horizontal picture. Finally, he could walk easily.

But during the worst of the vertigo, when his head swam the most, Norman researched the history of dizzy spells. He learned about Prosper Ménière's Syndrome (1799–1862); and the French filmmaker who called himself La Ménière, because he suffered from severe vertigo for thirty years–from repetitive paroxysmal vertigo. But even stranger still, La Ménière spent his entire career in a serious pickle. As a young man, he managed to find a loyal backer named Labrouste, a gentle laconic commodities investor. Labrouste's blind trust led to a very unusual contract. He would pay La Ménière everything up front, entirely before shooting began. Then when the film was done, La Ménière could itemize his budget, and return any unspent money.

For a few early shorts, that worked fine, but then Labrouste died unexpectedly, leaving no time to arrange his estate. So their unusual contract remained as part of the will. Legally La Ménière inherited a special fund, but could lose all of it, every franc, the moment that "he actually finished" a film. He could drag out his pre-production work, rewrite for years, shoot and edit for a decade, even "nearly complete" as many films as he liked—and for each, draw another fifty thousand francs. But the moment any proof came to the heirs that he had actually "finished" a movie, they would set dogs of hell upon him.

So the legend grew about a secret cache of film cans, with movies about vertigo. Had La Ménière actually completed a dozen films? Was this five minutes by La Ménière the end of that two hours? Cults searched for secret premieres of his work, like alien sightings. Then clues to one of them caused a stir. Perhaps the reader has seen the article recently by Goldblatt on La Ménière's "unfinished" masterpiece: *Freud in New York.* As the movie opens, we see Freud struggling with vertigo, lying on the Persian rug on his famous couch. We enter his POV. Vertigo literally "uncoils" through traveling mattes. Strands of brain tissue rise in slender filaments, like floating gold leaf. Then Freud goes to the conference at Bremen, and by boat to Manhattan. There, for over an hour of the film, he is trapped in a sexual farce about phobias among New York socialites. One orgy leads to another, sexual penetrations pile up like vertigo inside an eloquent recreation of a Manhattan hotel circa 1909. Finally the director, La Ménière himself drops from the ceiling. We see him in his familiar rumpled tuxedo. He screams obscenities at the camera. The camera follows him picking up the last two minutes of the movie, a tail of celluloid a hundred feet long. Cackling like a rooster, he sets the last two minutes on fire. Soon the movie frame itself starts to burn. Flames literally engulf La Ménière. He escapes by slithering up the wall, almost like a lizard, and disappears.

Recently, the heirs have gone to court, to argue that this is an ending. But for Freudian ephemerists, it may be a beginning. Folio 7 proves La Ménière correct. In the passage leading to the Coney Island episode, Freud writes that he and Fliess did indeed suffer occasionally from vertigo, from "dizzy nerves" caused by stress. Of course, can we trust what anyone, even great figures, write about their afflictions? Freud also added: "When vertigo took me over, grains of truth just slipped through my fingers."

In 2004, Norman introduced the Sim-Freud problem to the German filmmaker Eckhart Schmidt. That inspired Schmidt to began a screenplay. He is still trying to get Al Pacino to play Freud. The story opens with a perverse angle of the Statue of Liberty. From there, an ocean liner zooms in on Freud, Jung and Ferenczi at the bow, trading insults and insights, like Cole Porter songs about therapy. After the opening credits, we enter a swank 1909 libertine world, from Fifth Avenue to Harlem. Bits of business overlap. The master scene unfolds. Bawdy hostesses try to coax Dr. Freud into playing the rabbi at orgies, to deliver the hard truths about their afflicted lives. Reluctant to be a seer for these idiots, Freud struggles to find a moment by himself. He escapes with Jung to Coney Island. After gloomy but comic encounters, we follow him running like a tottering older man down the beach. He drops his cigar on an oil rag, and through a chain of sparks, accidentally sets fire to Dreamland.

It is like Orpheus in slapstick. Freud descends into a farcical underworld. Amazingly enough, production has indeed begun. An imaginary Coney Island has been built in Munich, mostly indoors. At Babelsberg, near Berlin, a faux Manhattan will double as Vienna—only a hundred meters from the famous Caligari Halle, where the German Expressionist film industry began in 1919 (now a skating rink). Throughout the orgy scenes, even one set on the ice, with music and Viennese rag-time dancing—as New York turns into a cross-dressing erogenous zone—Freud is plagued by an attack of vertigo; much the way Schmidt was struck by vertigo in 2002. What's more, various crew members claim that they hear voices from dead relatives. But a nervous grip (who refused to give his name) said that "movie sets are always infected with psychic rumors. It's as common as overdoses. Half the cast is usually possessed by something expensive and exhausting."

Indeed, the ninety years of coincidence that link Sim-Freud to seemingly everything must be seen as historical, not psychic. We cannot let Jungian or Rankian mysticism confuse us here. Years before Schmidt's movie was even imagined, back in 1999, Norman Klein introduced Sim-Freud to media artist and theorist Lev Manovich. While meeting for overpriced coffee at the Beverly Hills Hotel, they both decided to translate the story into an ironic data pilgrimage. They would let Sim-Freud span the entire twentieth century. Odder still, they met precisely one month before the discovery of the *Ephemera* was announced at a conference in Rotterdam (where Edgar A. Poe pretended that Hans Pfall was first sighted, after a flight to the moon, in 1835). Over the course of a weekend, Klein and Manovich concocted a data narrative, called it *The Freud-Lissitzky Navigator*. Lev went to work designing it. Much of the text stayed in Lev's Russian-inflected English, like a ghostly filter.

Meanwhile, Norman heard the ghost of his great-grandfather M+K rising to complain. A rasping sound, vaguely like a human voice, ached in the back of his head, as if a synapse were pressing against a nerve. This was not the first time. Back in 1967, a hippie mystic in Montreal had warned Norman that his great-grandfather bore a grudge. The mystic spotted Norman doodling, then walked up to him.

"You have lived in two worlds and are lost in a third," he explained. Norman vaguely agreed.

Then he added: "Your great-grandfather danced in Europe. He is angry with you, perhaps unfairly, but you must do something." Norman was supposed to leave the doodle under a tree, and pour a glass of water over it—that weekend or never at all—to soothe the old man's nagging spirit.

Of course, Norman forgot to bother with all that, simply overslept, even lost the doodle altogether. Afterward, his emotional life was lost at sea for twenty-five years. Electronic equipment often crashed, even went on fire spontaneously, when he sat near it. His strange luck became a running joke. Finally, belatedly, late at night in 2004, he offered this novella to M+K. It was nearly three in the morning when he decided. He set his mind to conjuring up a picture. He imagined an old man trying to never go back to that dreary farm. Legend has it that when M+K was ninety-seven years old, he would sit near the kitchen, waiting for women to pass by, then reach for a last squeeze of their hips, to restore his intimate memories before it was too late.

Feeling a trifle silly setting paper on fire, Norman listened for M+K's voice. A groan under the floor awakened. Something like a voice spoke in a very foreign language that Norman, never good at languages, still understood. It was a rare pleasure. The voice told him a secret about his father, of Young Yussell's first encounter with a prostitute provided by M+K in Hungary. Yussell's penis was so cold from waiting outside, he was embarrassed, needed help; and for a moment, thought prostitutes knew how to make men happy, would be patient with him. M+K made Norman promise to never put this story in print. But Norman has clearly decided to break that promise.

Of course, that's Norman speaking, not me. I will maintain scholarly objectivity to the end, even the middle. And as long as my medication holds out, I am a man of Apollonian good spirits, not a neurotic who keeps confessing (but lying) to strangers, as Norman does. You undoubtedly have read about that unflattering incident in Canada, near the ancient forest. His passport has finally been restored, but it took some legal finagling.

I repeat, as I have said so often, it is nearly impossible in this culture to not erase your own identity. Think of what Freud's *Ephemera* has taught us, how little we knew before. Freud constantly erased exceptions to his theory in order to keep going. I am particularly fond of the five pages he called *The Psychopathology of the Stomach: Daydreams On How To Gut A Fish* (Folio 8, orange insert), with that Talmudic commentary on mushrooms (in a tiny handwriting); and references to young women who eerily resembled his wife when she was young, but with one feature improved—a better neck, or tighter hips, the nose sharpened, the thighs leaner. Or Freud's line about the stomach as dreamwork, where he discusses trans-pathologies inside the body (again, mentioning his "near hallucinations" when women's faces transposed while they spoke to him). Freud even wondered if the autonomic nervous system cathects like the mind, if the stomach could be part of the Id (*Ich*).

Of course, he scraps all this as nitwit chatter, along with his recurring dreams that "smell" of Coney Island. Mass culture must be kept at a safe distance, a blind parallel to consciousness, like the stomach. So too with media. In Folio 5, he writes: "I just had a grueling phone conversation with Dora. The telephone mummifies me. It dries out my flesh, but keeps the skin intact."

We return to 1909 in America, to make sense of this final clue: At last, a day after Coney Island, Freud got to see a wild porcupine. Abe Brill and Stanley Hall both made sure to find one. He was also mildly impressed by Niagara Falls (where the annoying comment, "Let the old gentleman go first" may have taken place).

Then accidentally Frida is told about about Sabina Spielrein (can Ferenczi ever keep his mouth shut? Or did Jung put his arms around Frida "poetically?"). With Sabina on her mind, Frida reads something very intimate to Freud on the telephone, something about therapy being a masturbatory pleasure similar to entertainments in Coney Island.

Here Freud's penmanship changes. In the margin, he doodles concentric "flesh-like" objects, perhaps sexualized telephone receivers (see Goldblatt again). We sense his infatuation with things that deliver "passionate withdrawal," eccentric distance. In 1910 (Folio 9), he calls the telephone "erogenous vapors."

While she chatters on, Freud agrees with Frida's "theories" once again; and it was not like him to agree that often with women in long-term therapy. He agrees that a Coney-Island attraction–where a thousand people watch themselves stripped naked, metaphorically speaking–is like a machine inventing desire. Whoever controls that desire might be able to "colonize primal process." But this is not simply pornography, he insists. After a pause on the line, Frida agrees with Freud, saying: "Yes, pornography is not as passionate as the machines in Coney Island."

Freud holds the phone for a minute after Frida hangs up, as if the electricity inside the receiver were completing her message.

Then he crosses something out in his notes, so thoroughly that even "laser searching" cannot quite lift it.

That brings me to another problem, about laserographic confocal search methods. You'll excuse my drift, but perhaps you are following the legal campaign against laser searches (LCSM) in the US and the European Union. What rights to privacy do the dead possess? I say none. (Norman worries too much. He probably thinks they need attorneys). He retells that story about Young Yussell opening a side of beef at the store. Ghosts used to rattle between the floorboards, like rats mating. Eventually, customers spread the word about the ghosts. Business picked up, making Yussell unconsciously nervous. He was afraid if he hired someone, the man could be a thief. So Yussell made customers pay a little extra to hear what the ghosts were saying. Apparently ghosts cannot keep secrets. They love to gossip about the living. Very soon, every customer's bad habits turned into a public joke. In less than a month, business went back to normal (except the week of Halloween). "For the dead," Yussell explained, "human problems are the only pleasure they have left. It's what they do for a living, the same as cutting meat from dead animals."

At first, you enjoy the public shame caused by ghosts. Your bad habits go on display. You and your close friends make fun of your naked truths. Replacing intimacy with embarrassment can be entertaining, like pornography. It becomes a simulation of therapy, an animatronic, behaviorist friend. In 1925, Freud writes about psycho-analysis being "watered down," like an entertainment. "Many abuses, mostly unrelated, find cover under its name. In America, too, psychoanalysis comes in conflict with Behaviorism, a theory which is naïve enough to boast that it has put the whole problem of psychology out of court."

It seems that Freud was the pot calling the kettle black. In the _Ephemera_, he lets us know what he was thinking while his patients talked. Now finally, we see what he wanted therapists to never show their patients. Then he links this to his Coney-Island PROUN (1926), a thrill ride modeled on the orifice at Hell

Gate, a haunting. He both admired and was haunted by these erogenous amusement parks for late Victorian Americans. He dropped hints regularly about "moths flying against the screen," that therapists make fiction about their patients (a Coney Island of the mind, as the poet Ferlinghetti called it.) So we learn by what he said, not what he did in the *Ephemera*.

Like this "ephemeral" Freud, we irrepressibly need to confess, no matter how we block it out. We leave traces of the naked truth when we cover up. That is why fiction is more believable than objective fact. In everyday life, we condense our facts badly, project them, displace them, paint a black line to exaggerate an absence between things—pretend that we are hiding—fake history out of a barely remembered moment.

With the *Ephemera*, we see this fictive impulse turned utterly dialectical, a geometry of unspoken speech, and crossed out exceptions. Very soon, perhaps in five years, we may know too much to tell Freud's biography, to make it whole. Norman likes all this confusion, a bleeding through. He likes what the *Ephemera* has done. We are finding hundreds of Freudian unfinished pieces of business, Freudian bridges we never knew existed, until they were burned. The rush to find these exceptions is fast becoming an industry in itself: ephemerana. Forty books on the subject, and over two hundred web sites, will be out by the end of the year.

But now comes the question on everyone's mind: Who will be "ephemerized" next? I hear rumors about Jefferson's writing closet, even "uncoveries" in the correspondence of Marx and Engels. We're the ghosts doing the haunting now. But do we really need to hear every belch and feel every sexual urge that humanized these icons? The answer, of course, is absolutely yes. It is the only way to update, much less recover, our sense of a subconscious life. A globalized Coney Island has long since displaced our sense of intimacy.

The Last Straw (Mechanized Ghosts): Norman thinks that the next generation of "ephemera uncovery" will save us from us all that. The peel will become molecular, something called "nanoscopic" search, an almost theological science. Apparently, sound and speech can be recovered nanoscopically. A sound never actually goes away; it simply lowers its reverberations, even for decades. It is possible to hear (or scent) what was said, like a dog sniffing the presence of someone who walked by days ago. This is what Norman means by ghosts, what his family has meant for generations. They are the traces of sounds. A few unlucky souls hear them, even think they can talk to them.

The scientific theology behind all this seems too close to fiction to be fact. The space between atoms is not silent. Thousands of eccentric vibrations, called "phonons," are trapped by each molecule. Researchers claim that phonons are particularly "noisy" inside the brain, but are found in all matter. Think of them as vibrating memory, as echoes, even of unspoken thoughts.

Vertigo heightens our sensitivity to these echoes. Once vertigo throws our canals off balance, it makes us dizzy with the buzz of lost sounds. Patients with vertigo often complain of a cochlear irritability, a heightening. La Ménière claimed that he could hear noise in molecules, in his blood, in his pituitary gland. It might be true.

Thus, vibrations in a molecule do make a noise, called a "startle." Nanoscopists have begun to record it. This sound registers as a signal in the membrane of the ear. Sounds can even be stored in the DNA of a piece of wood, like a chair or a ceiling. On the nanoscope, they look like a bubble in polymer; the bubble becomes "a visible sign" to molecules nearby. This vibrating "startle" buzzes a signal; it literally delivers a message to other molecules, fainter each time; but that can't be helped. There is has no way to stop molecular sounds; they are an infinite confession.

Strands of phonons–molecular sounds–tend to cluster, like dust. They will gather on anything, from organic to inorganic. Thus the centuries-old debate over whether a stone can think has now been solved. From water to rocks, memory can gather as a kind of vibrating lichen, a thought without life.

These clusters may fill a room ("haunt it," the nanscopists

say), but they also can strike the inside of the ear. When that happens, our brain decodes the clusters as words, as echoes from a ghost. They may not be words that you have ever heard (talking in tongues, etc.), but you will understand them nonetheless.

Phonons are microscopic drum beats that pass for words. They can be struck on any surface. When they vibrate into the brain, they translate into a rhythm, a musical language. These words sound like a ghost, even though they are little more than excess kinetic energy. They are motile; vibrating bubbles in the flux. A subway vibrates far below ground. The sound echoes in our shoes. We turn the echo into language: We sense that we have missed the train.

Evolution tends to favor animals that can sniff out these sounds, "scent" phonons. Humans are the exception. They tend to single-mindedly shut out this noise. As Freud discovered, we censor or filter these urgent traces of memory, particularly in our sleep. At the same time, humans are tantalized by these sounds, as if they were an erogenous zone, what some call "the siren effect." Clusters of molecular sounds excite our senses, even terrify us, but also seduce us. They are the puzzle left by a ghost. They speak, but generally in fragments, as in a dream. They rarely complete the sentence, the point of the words. Humans feel driven to complete the meaning instead; we are bred to do it, like a dog is bred to hunt, or fill a hole. When a molecule vibrates a meager phonon that only molecules can decode, the human brain doesn't care. It will go to great lengths to complete it anyway–by instinct. Human beings have evolved a unique skill; they can imagine completeness, even when it is not there. That skill to misremember and misspeak has grown the size of our brains. It makes us intelligent enough to outwit animals with powerful jaws. In all the world, we may be the only species that can make fictions out of absences, that can pray to a molecule.

As with all new media, the theology surrounding nanoscopy will pass soon enough. Utopia lasts until the investors move in. Then it transforms into another violent business, another

WMD. But "nano-sounding"–as it is called in the defense in-dustry–may also overload us psychically in valuable new ways. (I don't share Norman's hope that phonon overload can protect us against ourselves. Apparently, when too much memory is re-pressed, the overload causes migraines and strokes. Like avoid-ance therapy, Norman thinks headaches can put an end to the history of forgetting). But since Freud's day–symbolized by the nervous buzz that got to him in Coney Island–we have lived in variations of overload. They make us anxious, turn us violent, then and now. They are clusters of dynamic sound that we scent like a dog hearing an earthquake, like a Boccioni painting of the city vibrating (1910). This overload will now be industrially engineered. We will all become ghosts.

Over the next decade, we enter the age when phonons left by the dead may be harvested, going back up to two hundred years, through nanoscopy. That is intentional overload. It is the next fretful step in the era launched by the discovery of Freud's *Ephemera* (1999). Very soon, we will ephemerize traces from a thousand people in the way that Freud did for himself. The bleeding through has begun. At the same time, the era preced-ing nanoscopy has ended. Its beginnings and its conclusion were earmarked by Freud and his *Ephemera*, by the screen that he used to keep his memories private. Now, in place of isolated Coney Island noise, a new feudalism is growing in the United States, as I said earlier, dominated by a globalized Coney Island, by machines that harvest and industrialize collective desire. It is an industrial form of "the invaded unconscious," something Freud absolutely refused to imagine, except perhaps on his death bed, at the start of World War II. But now I repeat my-self, like the sounds in a molecule, ever fainter each time. I am dreaming on my feet, caught in a crowd.

Introduction

Let us begin this chapter with a slight exaggeration: After years of entertainment overload, we have lost faith in what used to be called "the unconscious" (except, of course, to help us shop). Presumably, we no longer need an unconscious anyway, not medically, not even legally. Unconscious obsession was just another Victorian hoax, like Freud in Coney Island. We're on stronger footing now. Our HMO's have proven that psychoanalysis is a colossal waste of good money. All that we really need is great medication. Three sessions should be enough to find the perfect buzz.

However, that still leaves epic levels of anguish underneath. No matter how smooth our anti-depressants—even with ideal roughage in our diet—we still worry ourselves to death. We sense a looming sadness, a void. Our hands rummage around for the genetic location of this sadness. We find a hole about fifty feet deep, down the center of our head.

Perhaps it would be fairer to say that global entertainment has presided over a loss of intimacy in our culture. Of course, there is no way to clinically prove that. Tracking polls aside, the "collective state of mind" is an imaginary construction. Psychologists identify "a profound mood" of moral disengagement, a growing distrust of all public culture. Many economic protections that we took for granted are caving in. As a result, countless Americans are in a low-grade nervous breakdown much of the time. They are expected to keep it to themselves though. They know that sadness is often chemical, like water on the brain.

In much the same way, entertainment can be over-the-counter medication. It neutralizes painful facts. But how precisely, as psychological theater, does it do that? This goes beyond entertainment, even to the way we all theatricalize death; and distort our memories, as fun.

Media theory is inundated with stories about "the blur between fact and fiction." This blur has damaged our elections, even invaded our personal lives (certainly mine). At first, the idea of blur sounds exotic, like a mystical journey, a surrealist disjunction, a drug flashback in a crime movie. But our version is just banal, a new twist. What's more, the blur has apparently been widening, like a crack in the plaster—in stages, since 1955.

By now, it is easier to call "it" a "place" instead of a blur. I imagine a phantom city sailing quickly over water. The steel prow is held together electronically, no rivets, only data. Last sited, it stretched across three continents. It sails uncontested through national and international waters, flying colors linked to global entertainment.

It is our ship of state, a trans-local nowhere, a not-to-be-found government. It can pierce anything solid, go straight through concrete. It can become a vapor, float into a room, enter the fluids in your body. Medically speaking, it brings on symptoms that vaguely resemble autism. The patient loses the sense of touch, feels overloaded and deprived, overstimulated and desensitized.

This new economy is psychologically very invasive, though it pretends to only want our consumer dollars. Then entertainment turns gloom into catharsis, into medicated theater, filled with special effects. A sexy lie is worth the money.

I am an historian of special-effects theater. In 2004, I completed a book on scripted spaces from 1580 to the present, on how power operates in illusionistic environments, like casinos, malls, computer games, even presidential elections. It was written as a very public story, about special effects as policy, ideology, collective misremembering. In casino light, the gambler pretends to exercise free will in a world of absolute predestination. It is a cheerful parody of individualism and democracy.

But there is another side to special effects. In this book, we enter its psychological aspect, as a symptomatic journey, with clues about our collective mental illness: the history of gothic revivals, of grotto effects (caves) so deep, they deflect light itself;

and a hundred more.

I particularly like the term "antechamber." For engineers of the ancient pyramids, the antechamber was often the last major room to be bricked in. As more interior places were sealed off, this central room grew into an exquisitely grotesque theater. It was the room to all rooms; it left open a path to all paths: to places for the dead; to places where servants were still alive; to a doorway from the pyramid itself into the blast of sun outside. Each path could be seen, but increasingly no longer taken, only watched, like a theatrical performance. The antechamber became cluttered with the last worldy and other-worldly things, not only with workers finishing off; but with leftovers from construction (the tools, as well as sacred objects not pure enough for the afterlife). People and irrelevant objects were stranded there, as if between worlds, like a grieving audience.

A flood of associations come with the term antechamber, toward what I call erasure and forgetting. I want to see where these connections lead, as fiction and fact, as the place between–a docu-fictive journey into the desensitized psyche. As I often say, our world may not be deep, but it is definitely shallow and wide.

Darker Memories of the World Between

For three days, my wife was starved to death. She no longer could absorb nutrition. The home-care nurse said that if she ate or drank, only the cancer would be fed. A drop of morphine on her tongue was all that she could handle.

While I felt profoundly guilty, and my vision was probably clouded, her final hours–as her body evacuated her, but her mind stayed alert–have stayed with me almost every night over the past year, over the past three years actually.

Most of all, she obviously wanted to linger another few days. In the mornings, for thirty minutes at a time, she would revive from her near coma, and become very clear-headed, cheerfully willful, quite present, answer questions, even tell a few one-liners. After all, this was a warm place. Her dearest friends were lovingly beside her–and our son. Why leave?

Meanwhile, the Filipino night nurse began to hallucinate. First she tried to help my wife reconcile with me, find some peace for us both, after so much waiting. She claimed that her prayers had brought me. For ten long minutes, my wife and I chatted intensely, clearly finding some relief. I tried to stay close to her body, so that her vanishing eyesight might catch my face.

Then hours later, the nurse awoke angrily from a nap. God had just told her that my wife must now decide to stop living, simply "let go." If she fought to stay alive any longer, she was denying her eternal soul.

***

Twenty-nine years earlier, my mother died in a hospital, of essentially the same cancer as my wife, at almost the same age (perhaps a year older). With my mother, I was consumed by anger more than guilt.

My mother would sometimes pretend to die, as a theatrical performance exclusive only to me. My father would be at work downstairs, opening sides of beef at the butcher shop. Upstairs in her bedroom, she rehearsed all afternoon, sharpening her pauses and gasps. Finally, she heard the click of the lock. Her son, who each year loved her less, had arrived from school.

She called for me. As I looked on, her strange play acting began. Sometimes she would stiffen as if she were having a stroke. At other times, she would pretend to commit suicide. Like the partner in her sinister comedy act, I had memorized her hollow tones of voice, her gestures, the roll of her eyes. I knew how to bow my head, and mourn beside her, even though we both knew that she was healthy.

Then illness finally took her over for fifteen years. A few days before my mother died–in Brooklyn while I lived in Los Angeles–she found the strength to telephone me. Our talk began as usual, inside our sinister comedy act. She began with half-suicidal play acting, about my failures as a son. Then, lightening attacking her; her theatrical voice suddenly broke off. She could no longer perform imaginary deaths. Her fictions simply disappeared; I could hear them leaving. When her voice resumed, it was her alone; but the timbre, the grain of her voice had a piercing isolation, as if the years of bad faith between us were now bluntly apparent, now that the play was ending.

The certainty of her death coming soon made closure between us very simple. We reconciled (I think sincerely) in something like an unscripted way. I cried fiercely. For once I was able to answer her. I was thankful for that, though I had bizarre nightmares months afterward. I saw her descending a subway platform on Avenue U, from south Brooklyn into hell, as a character in the movie *The Exorcist*.

This brings up a problem that will return: Real-life melodrama is often too obvious for fiction (filled with weak metaphors, silly coincidences). That is why our memory improves the plot, to tell a more fictional, more believable story.

Recently, in the past few months, my own performance as a patient has begun. The taste of mortality has reached me. Until this year, I have generally been struck by comical diseases. They ached and I took to bed, but they were odd. I actually once caught a flu in my balls. Another time, I tore my knee trying to avoid a very fat woman sliding too quickly behind me on a balloon ramp after a crash landing in Chicago. Chest pains brought on by sadness and tension felt like rushing (mock) heart attacks.

Then last April, another comical illness: While strolling with my son across the Brooklyn Bridge, as I hustled to keep in step with his long strides, I re-injured that airplane knee. This brought water along my leg that turned into edema during my flights to and from Norway (along with those wonderful helpings of Norwegian salted fish).

When I got home to LA, my hands began to swell strangely (another useless symbol, the writer afflicted literally in his typing fingers). This time, however, I actually have a disease, at first perhaps my kidney, now more likely a rheumatic condition. I feel the illness traveling through my circulatory system like a mouse in the wall. My body occasionally evacuates me, doesn't answer when I require improvement, not even with my new salt-free diet, and my endless exercising to restore circulation.

The disease is particularly vivid at night. My uneven sleep patterns are now punctuated by fierce nightmares, as I doze between the aches of my swollen fingers. There I dream of the final days of my wife's cancer; or the final long-distance call with my mother. I imagine myself choking to keep breathing, as they did. I begin to enter my own death watch, as if my body were telling me to "let go."

I wake up chilled to the bone, turn on the lights, walk to feel wood against my feet. But my nightmare is mostly theatrical, like my mother's, to remind me that there is still time (I won't die of a rheumatic disease). But it also deepens my bottomless sense of guilt, that I can never be forgiven, nor forgive myself. Most of all, my nightmares prepare me; they show me what my final moment could feel like, when no embrace, not even from my new loving wife, will pull me back into the room. Eventually I won't have a sense of touch, when it decides to shut down. But my thoughts will continue, confused I suppose.

I turn to check if morning light is showing through the blinds. The grumpy black Persian is asleep on the table beside my computer. She has some serious bowel problems, but doesn't seem very gloomy about it. Or is she? Who knows what a cat sees while staring out the window for hours at nothing in particular. Does something like a bad joke cross her mind? The sleeping cat and I spend two minutes not communicating (though I must say: a cat stood watch on my wife's bed while she passed, clearly sensed her body leaving).

Illness as Metaphor

I now have an illness filled with overworked metaphors, despite Susan Sontag's warnings. My sense of touch is literally being "erased;" I am being hollowed out by my immune system. Blood tests do not reveal any source for my condition.

Oddly enough, these exhausted metaphors work easily as social criticism–another place between, where metaphor substitutes for fiction: My disease is trendy, like a new hair style or tattoos. Statistics indicate that Americans are becoming more rheumatic. Perhaps this rheumatism is caused by collective sadness. Americans feel their immune system disappearing. Of course, this has happened before, trendy mental illnesses that seemed immaculate, without physical cause.

In the late nineteenth century, millions of people suffered from neurasthenia. It was the culturally apt disease of its time. Its symptoms were brought on by excessive modernity (quite vague symptoms at that, one size fits all). Weber had it. Bergson had it. So did Willam James, Dreiser, Edith Wharton, Proust. Thousands of middle-class bored women were struck mute or paralyzed by it. Freud treated dozens of neurasthenics. Simmel had sociological theories to explain it.

But doctors could not find physical causes, only the symptoms: deep depression, fatigue, a nervous distemper, an imploded, tight-lipped stillness, what Simmel called "the blasé personality." In short, your body was overcome by the speed of urban crisis. Its "overpressure... increased expenditure of cerebral activity," leading to "cerebro-spinal" shooting pains (called Rachialgia), as well as edema of the eyelids, quivering unstable legs, anemia. In some cases, victims were literally paralyzed by its velocity, by the windswept tension of the high industrial takeoff.

In the thirties, neurasthenia disappeared from popular medical discourse (except perhaps in the American south). Its symptoms were variously replaced by psychoanalytic terms, particularly "neurosis," often identified with the same kind of melancholia–for example, in 1910, already linked to catalepsy, neuralgia, spasms. Once again, there was no determinant inside the body; this was a socially conditioned disease.

By 2000, the term neurosis also lost its importance, even in TV sitcoms. Medical research then isolated new terms for essentially the same problem. New metaphors indeed took over. Psychoanalytic modernity was out. Freud, in particular, became a hermeneutic myth. There was probably an unconscious, but a subliminal, neutralizing place, not as haunted by painful traumas as Freud assumed. In the unconscious place, fact and fiction blurred, as well as work and play. It could be very counterproductive to sponsor this fragile place very much.

Here is a grab bag culled from recent literature:

> It is increasingly difficult to maintain barriers between work and play. Freud's dichotomy between psychosis and neurosis is no longer recognized. Instead, researchers should separate diseases of the ductless glands from those of the psyche...

> Transference and projection in talk therapy can be destructive and inhibit the patient. Neurosis makes a worker feel psychologically inadequate. Do not be a victim in the (Freudian) search for the release of tension.

Introspection is old-fashioned, like those laughable magazine covers from the fifties: "Wallow an hour each day in your worries—it helps" (*Psychology Today*). It can make you narcissistic, borderline and obsessive. Do not be a victim. Regulate and desensitize anxiety through drugs.

That is now our dominant metaphor: you need "medication." Upload, keep your overtime, and avoid sick days. This solution works splendidly for the pharmaceutical industry; and helps combine medication with the world of entertainment.

It also highlights some diseases; those that play off our fascination with the overmedicated, detached psyche. They literally resemble overmedication. And they are not contagious, not pandemic. They are immaculate—mysteries seemingly without internal causes—like neurasthenia a century ago.

From the popular medical shows, I have identified four diseases often lumped together for their auto-immune, disengaged symptoms. They each emphasize how medicated (benumbed) the psyche can get: clinical (chemical) depression; new trends in autism among adults; rheumatic arthritis; and Parkinson's.

The symptoms for each of these presumably turn our bodies into neutral receptors. Disease seemingly arrives by satellite, like a collective "globalized" loss of immunity. Of course, this is media hype. Besides, most of these illnesses are not mysterious at all. For example, around 2003, many American children were suddenly diagnosed with autism due to mercury poisoning. Then it was discovered that as babies, each had received too many vaccines laced with a mercury preservative. Infant autism is more like a pharmaceutical disease. Similarly, Parkinson's among adults may be linked to garden pesticides and rooting hormone compounds.

But the symptoms easily suggest a life incapable of a Victorian unconscious. They suggest our collective fear of being hollowed out. But then again, as I explained earlier, who can calculate the loss of intimacy among Americans, even if it is true? Suppose many doctors became extremely used to prescribing lots of drugs. A druggy neutralizing effect is increasingly a social good. For many, myself included, it replaces lost immunities. What then is the contagion between collective anxiety and popular medical practice? In one way or another, pop medical terms become metaphors in the war against invasion, loss of identity.

Shall we compare this to popular science fiction about a psyche invaded by medication, where every outsider becomes an intruder, as in a Philip K. Dick novel perhaps? Or to Dick's hallucinations while on speed? Or we can apply Michel Foucault's logic: The way a culture treats the insane is a clue to its fear of madness. Similarly, the way a culture prescribes drugs is a clue to its fears about intimacy.

Over the past few months, I have been struck hard by an autoimmune condition, with all the so-called trendy symptoms. My body literally entered a space between—an antechamber. Like a case of identity theft, my blood system and even my bones refuse to answer me. Last night, the symptoms grew worse, literally chills along my temples, similar to those Freud describes in the *Ephemera* (Folio VI.3, p. 256). "Fevers at night literally separate my body from the mind. My body steadily disappears, refuses to answer, while the mind lingers. The first light crosses the room. Our mind sits up in bed, acts like a filing clerk, taking

46

stock of merchandise that is missing."

As Freud suggested, during his own trials with disease, "once we feel our body deciding to leave us," we need to entertain ourselves "theatrically." That was his solution, practically what my mother did. He felt that we should remember irrelevant details, keep an emotional distance alive, exaggerate the space between (*der Raum Dazwischen*). I am reminded of someone I knew, between bipolar episodes, endlessly recalculating the interest on mortgages, for hours at a time.

"We sense a remorseful ache in our shoulder," Freud added, "a last touch of kindness, while our grip loosens over our body." Or we entertain ourselves with comic daydreams–the comedy of how we almost lost our money, almost lost our sex appeal, lost our way home in bad weather, lost the keys to the house while a fire started in the kitchen. "We watch important messages slip out of our hands."

This last comment from the *Ephemera* (Folio VII.4, p. 319) is often discussed; but not as much as the sentence after it: "Then at last, along the way, we even think of something sincere about God."

Years later, Freud returned to that page, and scribbled weakly in the corner: "As the old expression goes, ashes cleanse the palate," one of my favorite phrases from the *Ephemera*.

Fictions Between Bouts of Fever

No ashes cleanse the palate like a good murder mystery. Between sweaty naps, I rummage through my office. I find a rare clipping file kept by LA journalists of their favorite murders from the year 1959. The literary tone is perversely funny, very theatrical, about men being "slugged," or women found "semi-nude." Descriptions of cause of death are so hard-boiled, they are darkly funny today. Precise bullet trajectories into the brain pan, resemble baking recipes. Arrows show exactly how the body bounced off the cement. They remind me that on film and in literature, murder is best served in dim light, almost as a bad joke; with one corner left completely blank, to give the viewer a comfortable peephole.

The more convincing a murder looks, the more a bit of whimsy needs to be added, like the close-up by LaMénière where a parrot talks to a bleeding corpse. Or LaMénière's police sergeant at a crime scene in *Nowhere Fast* (1962), who suddenly declares: "To see a murder clearly, I need a peephole. Otherwise, the crime feels too naked, not fake enough."

In class lectures about murder in fiction–when I cite Freud as a crime writer–I call this peephole "the Bridge," because antechamber is often too hard to explain. Looking across a bridge can feel very immersive, like an all-embracing fog; or very reductive, like a spyglass. But most of all, a Bridge is a staging area for the viewer, a psychological zone of safety.

The Antechamber (or Bridge): a carefully staged psychological drawbridge, waiting area or doorway. A stopover before crossing between two worlds. For example, in the movie *Twice Forgotten* by LaMénière, a street is designed to resemble the inside of a brain cavity. Or the hero, while driving, cheerfully daydreams of visiting his own funeral.

As fiction, the Bridge combines our worst nightmare with our fondest desire, at the same moment,. It resembles what Freud meant by dream work, but as a fictionally designed space, like an amusement park. It is a place for collective misremembering, where two competing special effects share the same place, at the same time. It is trauma camouflaged, but still theatrically put on display, as if we had it under control.

Watching Movies During a Fever

Movies often rely on bridge effects. In the opening to *Blade Runner*, a giant eye is literally intercut as a Bridge between sleepless LA in 2019, and the interior first scene, where a cyborg kills a nosy therapist at the Tyrrel Corporation. Like a Magritte painting from the twenties, we first climb through a window into the skull of the city. Then we find the same window takes us into the hollow skull of the cyborg (a replicant, a skin job). The cyborg has no childhood to remember. He answers the therapist's question about his mother–"Let me tell you about my mother"–by shooting him.

The Bridge can also be infinite panorama, with no end in sight. In *Lawrence of Arabia*, the camera pans slowly across an endless desert, a hundred miles larger than the seventy millimeters on the screen. Similarly, movie westerns repeat late nineteenth century photo panoramas of the Great Plains: the camera emphasizes the trackless wilderness. Or the camera gets lost in the trackless frontier of outer space, along the endless blackness on the way to Jupiter or the Moon in Kubrick's *2001*.

Or it provides a bridge to help us watch a murder. In the film *Under the Bridge* (1954) by LaMénière (another of his unfinished masterworks), the opening credits reveal an overhead of the sleepless city. Then the camera swoops under the Triborough Bridge in Manhattan, and wanders through a peaceable, working-class neighborhood.

Windows barely rustle with light. All at once, we see a man holding a camera. Then he trips on a crack in the sidewalk. That gives us time to peek comfortably through one window. There, we accidentally see a woman being murdered.

Her screams do not alert anyone, not even people who know her. It sounds too much like another family quarrel. Neighbors think she is entitled to her privacy. LaMénière begins his famous voice over: "Even if I could walk inside her head, I mustn't force her to open her eyes. Not if she wants to keep them closed."

All forms of theater, whether live or on film, place the audience on an emotional Bridge, a staged crossing. The fourth wall, so crucial to late nineteenth century theater, is not simply a framing device; it is a safety zone where nothing can penetrate–the actor reaches toward a membrane, but does not cross; like my mother reaching toward me while she pretended to be having a stroke. She essentially implied, in her performance, that my taking her hand was pointless, would have no emotional impact. Keeping a physical distance between us was crucial to her performance. She showed me that her arm had already left the room, was paralyzed by the stroke (her impersonation of a stroke). She had lost all sensation, but not the feeling on her shoulder and her neck. They still had a sense of touch. So I rubbed her shoulder.

At this point, I must clarify a vital difference: The Bridge or antechamber is not terrifying. It is "not" horror, not helpless damnation. Characters do not burst into flames, or find themselves sucked into a hole by demons from hell. The mood is more like a strangely intimate conversation, talking about death, at a moment when you see both the inside and outside at the same time. The afterlife and life share the same space. This is indeed different from horror, where you are stripped of all defenses.

On the Bridge, you feel safe. You flirt with death as theater. It is a dark pleasure, but then again, so are thrill rides. The first roller coaster (called a switchback) was originally designed to reenact a train crash. And yet, the train stays on track, leaves you safe and sound. Coney Island was filled with thrilling ways to pretend to die.

Samples of the Grotesque: The Garden Of Monsters

Like an amusement park, the Bridge can be architectural–a stone walkway between life and death, as in the famous story of the Alchemical Garden. In 1538, at the Italian town of Bomarzo, Count Vicino Orsini mourned the death of his wife. At last, to honor her memory, he transformed his estate into a pilgrimage about dying itself–theatrically speaking of course. He hired the garden architect and sculptor Pirro Ligorio to build what came to be called The Park of Monsters, completed by 1552, and based on the fantasy epic poem, *Orlando Furioso*, by Ludovico Ariosto (1516–1532).

For nearly four hundred years, the park was relatively hidden from the public. But today, it is flooded by tourists, who particularly want to see the stone doorway that appears in hundreds of flyers and Baroque picture books. The doorway has been shaped into a gaping mouth. It is the mythic sea monster Orc opening wide to swallow. In Ariosto's version of this myth, the Orc is given men to eat as sacrifice, prefers to eat men, but is tempted by women left chained to a rock.

The stone mouth is six feet high, with a snout that is part boar, part fish; with a comfortable stone seat inside, in the back of its throat. But the creature cannot see you. Since the Orc was blind, its eye sockets are black holes. But when you sit inside its yawning mouth, you see foliage outside.

You become an audience safe on a Bridge, having a mythic conversation about death. After all, Orc in Latin meant a bridge to the dead—originally the name for Pluto, the god of Orcus, the underworld, where souls were forced to migrate between death and life. Then came Germanic cognates of Orcus: In *Beowulf*, orcs are the walking dead, Grendel's relatives. In popular folklore by 1000 CE, the word Orc expanded to an all-purpose symbol for death sneaking up on you: goblins, dwarves, incubi, crawling things from graveyards, creatures that strangled you in your sleep.

But most of all, for centuries, even into the Renaissance, Orc meant an evil storm at sea. This monstrous Orc (also a killer whale) swallowed ships, women and worthy seamen. It wrecked the ship of state. Increasingly after 1350, this storm wrecked the material culture of feudalism itself. Seemingly year by year, the Orc moved closer to shore. It waited at the harbor's edge, and fed on ships entering, or trying to leave, from one world to the next. Or it studied women chained naked to a rock, like the beautiful Angelina in *Orlando Furioso*.

Your journey inside the Orc began in an antechamber (the mouth): First you were swallowed. Then you wandered inside its endless stomach—its labyrinth. But within this vast stomach, you lingered, not yet digested. You watched things die while you clung to floating wreckage. Most of all, you watched feudalism die.

Thus, the myth of the Orc suggested a theatrical pause, to allow the Black Death to pass overhead. You were saved by the Orc's thick stomach wall. You were not yet digested or drowned.

Then, the Orc myth was restructured during the era of the French Revolution: it was retooled to express middle-class yearnings. William Blake turned the Orc into a sex pot from the Romantic subconscious – a youth in revolution, "thick flaming, thought creating." Critics often note, of course, that Blake was drawing upon Milton's Lucifer. In much the same spirit, Blake's Orc is a dazzling serpent, with a fire-red carbuncle on his forehead. His cheeks have scales made of pearl, gold and silver. His armor, like a crocodile's, is filled with rare jewels. He sparkles at war, and rapes his own sister – a "mighty fiend," a Romantic demon lover.

I imagine Keats in Rome visiting sixteenth-century doors carved to look like Orcs. They frame monstrous faces yawning widely, about to inhale you for a pleasant afternoon. Clearly, they are bridges to put you at ease, not scare you. They are theatrical versions of a troubled soul. Certainly they were not supposed to kill you, or promise bad luck. They are darkly funny gags (*stravagante*), like Day of the Dead drinking bouts in Mexican cemeteries, to defuse our fears (like the pleasure of Tolkienesque orcs).

Finally, the orc is a bird skimming the water, comfortable between earth and water, as it hunts. On May 3, 1818, Keats writes to his friend J.H. Reynolds:

> Have you not seen a Gull, an Orc, a sea Mew, or any thing to bring this Line to a proper length, and also fill up this clear part; that like the Gull I may "dip" – I hope, not out of sight – and also, like a Gull, I hope to be lucky in a good sized fish.

Imaginary Murder

Tonight, I notice one of my fingers has suddenly gone numb. I walk to the corner, where my street has been transformed into a Hollywood version of Bomarzo. A movie crew has dressed it for murder, completely erased its neighborhood identity of course.

The murder, for the remake of *When A Stranger Calls*, will be across the street from a tiny evangelical church on the corner, a retrofitted Victorian cottage. Its faded "Jesus Saves" sign, with four letters missing, has been replaced with hot red neon, like the barrel of a smoking gun. Or as salvation against the chilling tag line from the film: "Have you checked the children lately?"

Huge arc lights have turned night into day. It feels like a bad parody of a war zone. The movie could be about laying tar at night for a landing strip in Iraq; or taking soil samples on the dark side of the moon.

The look I get from the crew is strictly business, as if they were rooting a sewer line. The waiting time between shots is too endless to be called cinematic. The street is busy enough; but the effect is a limbo, an architectonic antechamber–no longer a movie, no longer a neighborhood.

What does the movie set fail to show? The area is mostly Salvadoran and Mexican, with a growing number of Anglos. On the corner, every Sunday, the little church roars with chanting and tambourines, to a congregation mostly from Central America. The eighty year old woman next door feels invaded. She has been legally blind for decades, due to a medical oversight by the US government.

The church helps strangers, even the dispossessed. A few years ago, a homeless man with an almost undrivable motor home was allowed to park in front. One day, his brakes gave way, and he plowed into my parked car. Another day, his angry girl friend accidentally set fire to the van.

The sparks caught the branches of an old camphor tree leaning against the church. The fire department arrived late, but somehow, as if by miracle, the winds had shifted. The fire blew away from the roof, and did not spread it to the five other houses densely packed, and rising from the south.

The homeless man cried bitterly as the burnt shell of his van was flooded by the fire crew. His girl friend had already disappeared. He tried to linger in the neighborhood, but everyone forced him out.

I suspect that ten years from now, the area will begin to look mostly middle class. But for the moment, none of the late suburban amenities that you find in many newly discovered downtowns apply here. A few diehard taggers hit the same houses and streets every few weeks. The youth crime statistics remain high, but rental prices are forcing out many of the poor families,, while hundreds of Latino lower middle class families (many in the building trades) have bought small houses here.

Services remain meager and worsening, even while real estate prices have tripled in five years. But inside this movie set, one dusty poverty-stricken corner is all they care about, a good place for harvesting a murder, like ten acres of avocadoes that need picking.

I often write about movies as a form of erasure. Every semester, at least one student does a project on movie locations and movie stills. But tonight, movie sets are also architectural theater, an antechamber.

I spend half an hour trying to restore feeling to my left hand. Meanwhile, I hear trucks pulling out. The day of shooting is ending. The set has been stripped bare in less than an hour. But traces of the shoot remain. On Sunday, the sexy neon sign will be unveiled to the congregation at church. No one will mention that it was used to conjure up fantasies of murder. They will give thanks. I certainly can see their point.

Another familiar bit of theater complicates the night. I just heard four unmistakable gunshots, probably a few blocks further south. Then I heard women shrieking near my house. But over the years, these gunshots are generally distant enough to dull my fears; for me, this is not a crisis. I no longer react all that much.

Next I hear the police helicopter circling in the general direction of the shots, as always. Then a silence takes over. My wife calls neighbors, just as my former wife used to decades ago. Distant gunfire in a rhythm suggests one shooter, rather than random gunfire, which could mean a shootout.

Thus, the sounds of gunfire turn into another theatrical

bridge, oddly comforting. I think of Fabricio in Stendhal's *Char-*
terhouse of Parma, listening to the Battle of Waterloo in the distance. He stands in for all the theatrical murders that we see in
our mind's eye.

As I have written before, we are mostly witnesses "after" the
fact. We live just outside the frame of the film. But we fill what
we miss with fiction. For an hour or so, while the unexplained
gunshots are still vivid, a few people leave their houses to talk.
But generally, in the new Anglo enclaves where I live now, neighbors are less curious than twenty years ago. They are less inter-
ested in who shot at who and why, in the social fabric behind it
all. However, a dull rheumatic anxiety remains, like parts of my
hand growing numb.

Reawakened by some throbbing, I pretend that I have figured
out what the shooting meant. Four shots came from one gun,
very loud, more like a small cannon than a pistol. They were
delivered evenly (calmly); and' were not answered. I imagined a
scenario like this: a young man has been knifed. Afterward, one
of his friends sends out a warning, like a funeral salute.

Immune Systems

The doctor told me, in so many words, that parts of my immune system have turned against me. They now attack my body,
particularly bones along my wrist, as if I were the intruder. Of
course, most diseases are mistakes in our construction. We are
clumsily made, with flaws in our machinery. Anti-bodies do not
know which is the invader, and which is the local team. Some
invading viruses sneak past the immune system by imitating
what the body considers normal. In my case, this rheumatic
over-reaction confuses the inside from the outside. It literally
brings ghosts into my room. Each night and into the morning, I
watch the zones of combat as if from an antechamber.

Hallucination

Between my snoozes, the new anti-inflammatory drug has just disconnected day from night, into yet another space between. Lots of time lost struggling to rest at all. The morning has finally arrived. My swelling drifts away. I sense a ghost waiting politely in the corner. She has none of that worm-eaten look that you see in movies. In real life, ghosts like to make a pleasing impression. They also chat continuously, give what sounds like good advice (though they're so out of touch, it usually turns out miserably). Ghosts understand our hollowing out better than we do, since they live evacuated from their body, in a state of sensory deprivation. Also, according to the newest paranormal research, ghosts do have life spans. Eternity is another of those hermeneutic myths, like pure form.

Like these ghosts, I would suggest that Americans are rapidly feeling more disembodied, through illusionistic theatrical spaces, in our public life, in our national policy of escapism—to medicate our political anxiety. Also like my imaginary ghosts, I sense the private time of my illness growing; the hours I spend watching its effects increase week by week.

National and Localized Forgetting

Today, a rheumy flu overwhelms me. I wake up with my body covered in a silly rash, like ants leaving a ship. I call the doctor, who tells me to suspend the medication. For three days, I dissolve into sleep so total, I finally begin to feel unhinged. At last, my hallucinations become more vivid than the house itself.

Like a prisoner who lost his deck of cards, I play solitaire by daydreaming (for hours) about psychic conditions in the US, compared to mine. My email crashes for the thousandth time. To keep diagnostic "help" on the phone, I mask my anger when I complain. The voice on the line copies a Midwestern accent. She has been named Suzy by the company; she lives in Bangkok, and wants to reboot my entire system. I hang up before she can, try another phone loop. An answering machine bumps me into oblivion.

Electronic devices are private enclaves. They shield the owner from anything like a direct confrontation. When you finally get through, disembodied voices violate your immunity. Of course, many Americans sense their immunity dissolving a little more every day, because American corporations increasingly treat them like aliens.

But to keep us medicated, the entertainment economy promises more forms of safety, of detachment. Every Christmas, it radically increases how many versions of privacy we can buy. So I have a theory: I would suggest that privacy is not intimacy, but rather making yourself harder to find. In a similar way, our auto-immune symptoms "help" us watch while our immunity disappears. We like being an audience in that way, I suppose–myself included–detached when the medication works.

As everyone knows, the middle-class home buyer (whoever that is) will pay serious cash for enclaving: sky-high real-estate prices, powerful cell phones, answering systems, internet dialogues, over-controlled parking, gated communities, private police, private schools. All this comforts and protects, while the public sector continues to dissolve. Enclaving is a hallucinatory medication against an immune system that is failing.

The reasons are obvious to anyone struggling to keep a bank account. Classes widen. Power becomes more abstracted through media and global investments. The American middle class continues to shrink. In self defense, Americans try to add more armor to their daily lives.

But armor does not shut off the internal madness. Millions still buy into the Bush administration's rhetoric on terror, a theatrical fiction about frontier justice, from a ruthless, unjust gang of thieves. It feels comforting (presumably) to be scared half to death, because secretly we know better. This is the comfort zone that sells long-distance versions of terrorism (the faraway theatrical antechamber)–to hide the moral and political disaster, the ruthless waste. Americans are being sold an "exaggerated"

Communist scare from the fifties (not unlike a horror movie or a cowboy movie). But internally, I believe most Americans know that we are safer than the paranoid language suggests.

Frontier logic is old-fashioned Freudian projection: our enemies are forcing us to hate them even more. They are soiling our good intentions. It is a familiar syndrome. Enemies are demonized beyond what seems accurate, to sound worse than they could ever be. That makes Terror perversely soothing, very theatrical, like an antechamber, like a faceless, unexplained, but "never truly" deadly condition.

This week, I am vaguely comforted by these endless blood tests. All of them show nothing abnormal in my body. This is not unusual for rheumatic conditions: immaculate symptoms without causes. My symptoms are faceless–my metaphor today for a global economy.

We live in an era of electronic feudalism, where unmonitored forces cross borders freely, steal freely, take away the immunity that Americans have felt. Indeed, we feel colonized by our own economy.

In the past, despite the cannibalistic nature of free enterprise, somehow the middle class seemed to keep growing. From 1948 to 1970, the American system promised and delivered for this growing middle class, no matter how many downturns took place.

Now, even the federal government is essentially allied with global interests, to strip away the "safety net" from the middle class. But this is not supposed to worry us. We must remain cool, unfazed (if we're lucky, untaxed), and worshipful of private wealth as the only protection against the evils globally out there. Thus, in a bizarre way, the War on Terror feels more under our control than the economy itself. Patience is its own reward.

***

The mail arrives. I receive a package embalmed in tape, a scholarly memoir from a man who I have known for almost ten years, who is now famous as part of a national scandal. It is obviously the next chapter to the antechamber–a comical and gothic Da Vinci code for Freud in Coney Island. There is no point squeezing it into what remains here. I'll have it ready in a few weeks, take us there next.

Leo is caught in a pattern familiar to all of us, when events detour so idiotically, we feel like a walking fiction. Everything serious that we try turns into farce. Everyone we meet is painfully careful with us. Every day, people act as if we missed the rehearsal.

He has been a "gypsy" scholar for forty years now, never tenured, in a hermetic struggle to remain solvent, through grants and occasional teaching. In 1982, he started CIM, the Center for Imperfect Memory, at a store front in Los Angeles. Located only five blocks from the famous Museum for Jurassic Technology, CIM became another local oddity, featured but rarely supported, in the LA Weekly. Leo was even flown to Germany once to lecture on the psychic collapse of America.

Then he acquired Freud's *Ephemera*, quite by accident, at an estate sale. Until that point, he had always been extremely detached and scrupulous-- and unbelievably tall, like a spotted giraffe. He would try to calm you down by stooping, but his huge head (with long black tongue) was suddenly right in your face. And yet, he never so much as raised his voice in public.

Today is different. He just yanks the microphone out of my hand. This morning, he acts like a boiling pot of coffee.

***

So I hand it over to Leo. "But to begin," Leo explains, "let me back up for almost eight hundred years:"

***

In 1288, a sentence by an unknown Arabic scholar (badly translated from the Chinese), caught the eye of the young Duns Scotus, during his studies at Oxford. And while Duns Scotus judiciously kept it out of his writings, he loved to toss the sentence into conversations. Later in his life, when asked by papal authorities where it came from, he falsely attributed it to Peter Lombard. That is as far back as our research can go.

The histories of this sentence took us fifteen years to assemble, and considerable sacrifice. We have located 611 variations since 1288. They make us wonder about the chicken and the egg. We are now convinced that the original meaning read as follows:

"False memory will bring virtue, but only if you treasure imperfection."

Of course, to honor this sentence, you must translate it falsely. Each translation must deviate, no two alike. That became the tradition for centuries. By 1624, twenty three of these "loose" translations, called "*truncatio*," were listed as heresy by the Inquisition. Nevertheless, deviations continued to circulate, always in new ways. As late as 1723, the most famous *truncatio*, known as "Imperfect Jesus," was cited in two hundred witch trials during the recapture of Hungary by the Hapsburgs. From Hungary, it passed to Germany, and to Alsace, then to Prussian immigrants hunting for treasure at the California gold fields in 1849. Finally, on September 14, 1896, another "Imperfect Jesus" emerged –unsigned–on the front page of The *San Francisco Chronicle*. Entitled "Imperfection: A Story that is Mostly True," the article was edited, if not rewritten, by Ambrose Bierce. It follows an argument between two theologians in 1651, somewhere in Germany. One is a true believer, in fact an elder of the Inquisition. The other is a heretic, about to face a hanging jury. The heretic argues that Jesus died imperfectly–as a man. He died to prove that imperfection is the only path to salvation.

To argue for the heretic, Jesus appears on the ceiling, as a vision. His words ring out as clear as a bell. His voice invents language all over again, "like the wind speaking."

'To be a true Christian,' He says, 'be very human, above all. Learn the lesson of the Cross. I died as a man to teach you that imperfection is your only guide against false prophets.'

Then his voice changes register. Wolves suddenly moan inside the church, so gently that each man begins to weep.

'My Heavenly Father makes you forget. Thus He binds you

to the earth. Blind faith is not enough. Instead, you must study the world. That is why I lived here as a man. The devil can be revealed to you in no other way.'

My discovery of the Imperfect Jesus became the pride of our research. It also took us from medieval heresy into the Enlightenment. For example, in an unpublished note, the philosopher Berkeley explains why God asked Jesus to die as a man. If Jesus were merely perfect, Berkeley says, then humanity could never "mend itself."

This resembles the Imperfect Jesus in social-contract theory by Rousseau in his famous plea to the Bishop of Ardennes (1769). But most of all, it appeared in Edward Gibbon's letter to the woman who got away. That letter struck me the most.

In 1761, Gibbon tries to win back the love of his life—quite ineffectively, as it turned out. He writes to Sarah Churchod, asking her to forgive him; and to forgive his father, who had broken off their engagement. Her response was immediate. She burned the letter, but copied some it into her diary (famous for its inaccuracies, because she knew that her banker husband, Jacques Necker, liked to read it secretly):

My dearest Suzanne,

Before you misunderstand what my father has done, allow me a moment to speak. Think of the imperfect Jesus. Do not ask for perfection in this world...

...(At this point, she deletes something too intimate for her husband to see. We believe Gibbon was commenting on the imperfection of his sexual parts compared to hers. But soon after, he returns to high ground)...

...Even Brunelleschi was blessed with imperfect memory. Had he understood ancient Rome thoroughly, his great Baptistery would have turned time backwards. Instead of the Renaissance, architects might have walked in togas for two hundred years, burning incense at the Temple of Jupiter. We are grateful for Brunelleschi's poor memory. Indeed, imperfection can bring great virtue. Think of that next time you think of me.

This letter inspired me. It made good sense. As Gibbon said, false memory inspires high culture. I retitled the project "Greatness in the Imperfect Tense." I was buoyed for years. We reorganized over ten thousand documents. It took us eleven volumes to simply record them all. Finally, in 2003, *The Archive of Imperfect Memory* appeared, to a storm worse than any of us could have imagined. Along the way, we ruined our backs, and became perverse anti-positivists. I now require medication just to face how ordinary I am, a cheap byproduct of a bad idea.

And yet, while the pills do their job, I must put in a good word for the research itself. Every day that I spent buried at my desk, I thought I was in a spa. I entered the cracks inside great minds, watched how they forgot, how they misremembered the past, lied to their loved ones, became suicidally confused. Like the Imperfect Jesus, I loved them even more for their failures.

Sometimes painfully ordinary people turn bad memory into groundbreaking cultural work. Consider this passage about Gogol, poor soul, my hero: a genius, but ironically dim.

In 1831, the beacon of Russian literature, Alexander Pushkin introduces German Romanticism to the young Nicolai Gogol. Still only an aspiring writer, Gogol is indeed something of a greenhorn from the Ukraine. He has read very few books, is oddly self-absorbed, initially fails as an actor, then attaches himself worshipfully to Pushkin's every word. However, as was his nature, Gogol is inspired by not quite understanding what he hears. He "profoundly" misinterprets what Pushkin tells him. Instead of luminous gothic romances, he delivers quirky social parodies. Then to his amazement, they make him famous, a hero in fact, when they infuriate the Czarist censors. Almost by accident, Gogol invents the modern Russian novel.

Even years later, with the benefit of time and distance, Gogol still remains confused by his achievement. Finally, after a fitful conversion to a silly, lunatic fundamentalism, he starves himself to death. Among his final notes: 'For a time, I thought my imperfection brought me virtue.'

But like Gogol's life, our project went sour. What's more, like

Gogol, we accidentally broke the law in several places. Part of our research even inspired a man to attempt murder.

Even worse than that, our major grant turned into a failed marriage. I should have caught the signals ten years ago, but all my friendships come to grief very slowly for me.

For six years, we were renewed—no questions asked—by the Binkley Bole Foundation, or "Bi-Bo," as it is popularly called. However each year, their evaluation report grew slightly more irrational, like a slow-growing mold. Finally in 1999 came the first shock.

I can see now why a shock was inevitable. Bi-Bo was born under a hex. It was funded by two ruthless and unstable men, David Kay Binkley and Myron Bole. They agreed to combine their trusts to make up for a great sin that they shared, but kept well hidden. Then quite unexpectedly, in 1981, both men died three days apart, leaving very few instructions. Odder still, behind their back, the board at Binkley—and at Bole—were already planning how to spend the money. A Bi-Bo constitution "suitable" to the board was ready to go a week after the funerals, before either man was cold in the ground.

Bi-Bo is nominally headquartered in North Carolina, but essentially run through a rattletrap office in Santa Monica—an architecturally famous mistake, a so-called dingbat. On my first visit, I was shown the only window facing west, with its tiny crescent-shaped view of the Pacific Ocean—more like a glimpse—almost two miles away.

That office was reserved for the president of Bi-Bo, a man of infinitely superior taste in shoes, but not much else. What exactly qualified him to run a $1.1 billion enterprise, I never knew. The office itself was designed by one of LA's better known architects, Gerald Goines. But apparently the Goines blueprints were utterly violated. Along the roof, instead of deconstructivist irony, something like a comb from the head of a chicken was added. At the entrance, blunt windows trapped the afternoon sun, heating up the building mercilessly. Then, to make matters even worse, Bi-Bo covered the windows with even blunter cypress trees.

I suppose buildings, like dogs, sometimes grow to look like their masters. I know I have. Eight years into the project, after eight renewals, Bi-Bo hired a bean counter to check our accounts. The man prided himself on being relentlessly narrow-minded, and hypocritical. Despite legendary cost overruns at Bi-Bo itself, he demanded that we prove we were serious about cutting waste.

So we agreed to auction off some of our more dubious acquisitions. One in particular stood out as a mistake; it had not even been unpacked. Provenance indicated a set of nine wooden boxes, filled with hand-written memoirs, travel photos and ephemera. A committee of experts labeled these *The Travel Diaries of an Austrian Physician*. This doctor (an obvious hypochondriac) wrote about Greece, even spent a miserable holiday in New York in 1909, and so on. Since we had paid only $350 for the set, the bean counter advised that it wasn't worth the space it occupied.

At Sotheby's, the boxes sold with some difficulty for $900. Then a chasm from hell opened up. The new owner had the boxes reappraised, discovered that they were the personal *Ephemera* of Sigmund Freud, valued at more than $40,000,000. It was only the first in a chain of disasters.

All at once, my photo appeared in dozens of newspaper stories; I don't know why. I was officially the imbecile of the year. For a satirical art show called *Insipid Knowledge* (opening at the New Museum in 2000, then traveling the world), one artist made a scare mask out of my face (in the style of Bernini's bitter self-portraits) My face became so popular, copies were sold at bookstores around the world, even for Halloween.

Meanwhile, the German scholar who had convinced us to dump the Freud boxes was then promoted to chair of his department. And with headlines raging, the president of Bi-Bo (and four officers), vanished on a long "investigatory trip" to eastern Europe. After Christmas, the story still refused to die. So they added a "pilgrimage" across Asia, then one more month around the world.

We now know that the entire trip cost at least $405,000. To

justify their tax-exempt status, en route they bought a rare collection of Polish cigarette tins, a few art catalogs (possibly Hong Kong phone books), and twenty "school of Rembrandt" etchings, mostly to dress up the president's office.

But I won't clutter my report with Bi-Bo scandals. It might poison my chance of ever getting another grant anywhere. (I only hope that Norman Klein, our copy editor, isn't publishing this as another of his venomous jokes. Or worse still, editing as he pleases, putting words in my mouth.) I will admit to a few things: I did have unusual sex with a seductive vice president at Bi-Bo, as did three other winners of Bi-Bo grants. Some of the stories about her are true. Her body was indeed so completely rebuilt by plastic surgeons, she liked to call herself "a special-effects ride." You undoubtedly have seen the web sites (at least 2.5 million people have already logged on). Please don't give me any more grief.

Needless to say, the media frenzy around Bi-Bo has grown from scandal into permanent legend. Copies of my face are still bouncing off satellites, traveling to other galaxies. But meanwhile, painful as this is to admit, the president and his Bi-Bo illuminati will pass unscathed. Their contemptuous style is even trendy. Two "Bi-Bo's" have recently done American Express ads.

Of course, three other Bi-Bo's had to be sacrificed. As one headline read: the president "tossed three execs to the wolves;" but each left with a solid pension plan, and continuing health benefits. Americans respect loyalty among the rich. As for the highest echelon at Bi-Bo—the grand masters of chaos—they graduated to full professorships and deanships at major research universities.

And yet, even while my life keeps dissolving before my eyes, I cannot argue that Bi-Bo is badly run. After all, who can say precisely what Bi-Bo produces? To quiet the critics, Bi-Bo even set up an expensive competition on *The Future of Giving*, flew the jury to Hawaii, and voted itself "the best run foundation in America." Of course, that was the year–2000–when America rewarded many wealthy men for their complete ignorance, men who promised to never plan too far ahead, men who always sounded upbeat.

In 2002, the trustees at Bi-Bo hired an advertising agency to improve their brand. The result was magical. Eye-popping foldouts made the board at Bi-Bo look like Medicis.

But not me. To add insult to injury, I received a steady flow of threatening letters. The most dangerous came from a man named Gilbert Flucks, obviously a pseudonym. This Flucks claimed that Bi-Bo was destroying his "family and mental health." At first, we ignored his letters. Then Mr. Flucks launched against us directly. He claimed that he owned documents from the seventeenth century that made a mockery of our research. He wanted to publish them, and expose us as "Sanhedrin who killed the Imperfect Jesus."

His letterhead showed only a phone number and no address. The postmarks also kept changing—but always from somewhere in Los Angeles County. That meant anywhere within a thousand square miles. Finally, I tried to call him on the telephone. An unusually calm voice answered, more like a man with a strange hobby than a lunatic. He was so calm, I couldn't make out every word he was saying. The reception burst into strange noises or other voices, as if it were a party line from 1950. I only heard his last comment: "So now you have the gist of it." Then he hung up.

His next letter, postmarked that very day, thanked us for agreeing to publicly admit that our research was garbage, "to finally show some class." He enclosed three xeroxed documents. The first was a frontispiece from a small book published in 1608, of excerpts in Latin from Thomas Aquinas. Instead of a title, the famous quote from Aquinas dominated the page: *"Recta Ratio Agibilium"*

In official Catholic circles, this Latin instruction is broadly translated as "the true way applied to everyday life."

Also in the envelope were two photostats from 1648, both rather muddy, difficult to read, perhaps even worm eaten, or damaged by the weather. In each document, Flucks circled a word added to *Recta Ratio Agibilium,* destroying its meaning. In the first of these, the extra word seemed to be *oblivia,* or an adjective from *oblivascare*–to forget, or to obviate, as in oblivion. In the second, it looked like *curtus,* meaning cut short, defective, mutilated; or gelded like a horse.

We were forced to hire a seventeenth century specialist to check on these. A Professor Sauter told us that they were anti-Catholic statements (hardly a surprise), probably from the duchy of Alsace. They were parodies in a Neo-Latin slang common during the Thirty Years War.

Further down each column, Prof. Sauter found vivid descriptions of Catholic priests doing unspeakable things–mating and defecating like farm animals, because they were agents of the Catholic Hapsburgs.

This blasphemous Neo-Latin had been evolving for centuries among traveling priests and scholars, since the era of the Goliardic poets in the twelfth century, then after the popularity of Erasmus' Neo-Latin. The writers in this case were probably defrocked clergy: a group who condemned the Pope, but still practiced their own version of Catholic mass.

Then came more nails in our coffin: On various pages, other *truncatio* appeared, like owls at the window, more deviations on "Imperfection brings virtue." And beneath each *truncatio* were long, gruesome accounts of priests endlessly eating and shitting, while the faithful died of starvation.

These heretics were not simply attacking the Catholic Church. They were violating my life's work. How on earth had Flucks gotten hold of this "evidence?" Over the next few months, he sent us even more xeroxes, dated from 1647 to 1659, sixteen in all, one more besotted than the next. Rabelais would have blushed. The language was scabrous, scatological; it compared Papal morality to the smell of gangrene, to a leg that needed amputation. Then, from beneath these oozing sores, another *truncatio* would float to the surface.

He converted our research from a defense of high culture to

grease under a slaughterhouse. I needed to talk to this Flucks. But his phone stopped working altogether, was flooded by echoes, or endless overlapping dialogue. However, that didn't stop him from giving us a piece of his mind, on an audio tape.

"Any two points can make a line," he wrote, "even stupid points. As Lao-Tse said: 'Like an empty vessel, the virtue of imperfection is that it can always be filled.'"

He was convinced that the crucial source—the one that Gibbon and Berkeley knew—emerged during the religious wars from 1520 to 1660. By 1640, half-remembered Latin phrases turned into sick jokes about torture, about peasants trapped between hungry armies. *Recta Ratio Agibilium* now meant death on your doorstep, specifically the invasions of Alsace.

So there it was. I had missed the boat entirely. As of 1647, a cult of radicalized former priests from Alsace specialized in *truncatio*. They essentially turned it into Baroque punk.

And they invented prayers to go with their sacrilege—a mass called **le** *roseau*, the reed. I wondered if they were borrowing from Pascal, who often called his frail body a thinking reed; but the *Roseauistes* believed that plagiarism was God's work. They assumed that nothing is original, including sin. Even when they recorded local folk tales, they promised never to copy them accurately.

Do not assume that only human beings play-act. We have observed that sheep, after grazing, like to perform little plays for each other. They pretend that they are shepherds.

So it is with humankind as well. We try to copy God, but find glory only in pretense. We need to believe that the wind speaks Latin.

Thus, while my research grew more optimistic—I even taught a seminar called "Researching Pure Form"—Flucks went the other way. He came to believe that we were hollow shells. He called my work elevator music.

Then all at once, he stopped insulting me. He went after Bi-Bo instead. "Shit from the bowels of the earth," he called them. He sent me terrifyingly vivid documents, more inside dope on

Bi-Bo. I received xeroxes of their orgiastic expense accounts, lavish room service, including sexual favors. As Klein used to say: "He can see the pimples on their ass."

Then in March, 2002, Flucks began to go public against Bi-Bo. First he published in a small weekly newspaper: two letters summarizing Bi-Bo orgies on the road. Then the letters made it to cable news. And since no photos were allowed by Bi-Bo, my picture was featured again, like a bulls-eye.

Of course, I sent the Flucks xeroxes to Bi-Bo. As my grandfather used to say: "There is nothing more loyal than a one-eyed dog." I didn't realize that I needed those letters to protect myself legally.

Because the next week "they" came to the house. I have never met anyone from organized crime, but an hour with lawyers from Bi-Bo was probably close enough.

"We are considering filing suit against you," they said. "Legal action."

I imagined myself blindfolded on a road. Suddenly I blew a gasket. I can be rather overwhelming, like a great golem when I stand at my full height. I put one hand firmly around the tiny neck of a Bi-Bo lawyer.

The conversation took a different turn. I told them the little I knew. We checked for errors in their brief. I made a pot of green tea.

Afterward, Bi-Bo hired investigators to locate Gilbert Flucks. With their money, it took only three days. His real name is Gilbert Fleisch, or Bert. His surname Fleisch descends from a meat cutter who lived in Galicia, Poland (1764–1809). He is forty-eight years old, already retired, living with his family in a so-called "Tudor-style" house built in 1926. The house slouches more than sits on nearly an acre, mostly undeveloped brush up a granite slope, thirty miles northeast of Los Angeles; in one of the steep foothills above the town of El Monte.

Flucks bought the property at a sale eleven years ago, after a spring mudslide. The foundation is precipitous, dangling on a foothill. The garage also had a trail of violations that dropped the price another $100,000.

Flucks did not notice the garage at first, a grave mistake. It was immense, big enough for three or four cars, but it had a false floor. Below the floor was a mine shaft literally sixty feet deep. In 1971, the former owner, Ted Burroughs had discovered rare slate there, and began digging, then cutting tiles. To hide his secret business from nosy neighbors, he added a floor on hinges. Then he built scaffolding and ladders below that, a little more each year. Not until he needed to sell did Burroughs realize how far he had dug, how it looked to a building inspector.

Flucks saw the endless pit only after moving in. He was horrified. The disclosure had barely mentioned it. He sued Burroughs, and won another $100,000 easily.

Then Gilbert Flucks put his peculiar talents to work. He studied what could be done with a stone basement sixty feet deep. He became a homegrown excavationist. He collected dozens of subterranean designs, mostly unbuildable. He bought hundreds of books on "the unbuilt," on Piranesi, on the history of grottoes and the grotesque. All this drew him to the seventeenth and eighteenth centuries. He disappeared inside old manuals on Baroque theatrical illusion–on building the artificial and the imperfect. In 1997, he came upon my research, even visited CIM when I was out, another accident that came back to haunt me.

That $100,000 from the lawsuit did not last long. Flucks had already gone through half of it just hiring carpenters who could work sixty feet underground. He and his family lived almost hand to mouth. The only salary came from his wife, Athalie, who earned a pittance as a glorified secretary at Bi-Bo. However, in 1998, real estate prices started to zoom along the San Gabriel foothills. And that same month, Athalie received two huge raises at Bi-Bo, for services of a mysterious kind. A year later, she was promoted to executive assistant, and then to vice president in charge of grants for the arts.

The new money came just in time (refinancing and a Bi-Bo grant). Flucks began to order rare lumber to furnish his grotto environment. He particularly wanted woods that could "enrich" echoes. Unusual sounds were rising from below, and seemed in his mind to meet noises at the roofline.

In 1999, trucks unloaded almost 3,000 board feet of rare hardwoods, particularly green, Pumpkin and Blue ash–especially Mountain and Quickbeam ash, known as Rowan, the father of trees. Legend told him that Rowan builds a path between to the inner and outer worlds.

Months later, pallets of even rarer woods were delivered–to "consecrate" sound: fifty yards of alder, the wood of flutes; twenty yards of birch for cleansing; fifty of elder, the crucifixion tree for the Imperfect Jesus; twenty of hazel wood for seeking the voices of thieves and murderers. And most important, a lucky find: two hundred yards of ancient oak, from the floor of a recently demolished stable, built in 1685, near an ancient forest. And as a final statement: twenty yards of yew, to incite inner visions, to "make the bow that speeds the shaft."

That is how immersed Flucks had become. The Roseauistes had claimed that woods could speak. He added a library for his seventeenth-century Roseauiste library, their books of theory, incantations. Finally the entire garage was modeled on Roseauiste carpentry, a Baroque mix of sweat lodge and sound studio.

But what did Flucks want from me, or from Bi-Bo? After all, 1998 to 2000 were the glory years for the Flucks household. Athalie gave birth after only four hours of labor, to a cheerful little girl, Miranda, who luckily slept through the night after only eight weeks.

Flucks retrofitted a new foundation sixty feet down. The cement casing extended almost to the roof. On top of the cement, he installed lavish paneling. Then he began carving on the panels, over fifty feet down, thirty fee above. Like Ulysses, he wanted to hear voices; and so he did.

By 2000, he had turned his obsession to Bi-Bo itself. Apparently, he had just discovered that he had become agoraphobic. He couldn't leave his garage for more than twenty minutes at a time. His daughter would bring food to him every afternoon, and stay near him. But not his wife. He knew that his wife was having sex with Bi-Bo clients. She saw him as a lunatic, a Roderick Usher. But he was too weak to abandon.

She was, after all, his only mental connection to the outside. In what appeared at first a conciliatory tone, he begged her to tell him her stories, every indiscretion, every membrane of it. Some of her stories were very toxic to their marriage. Finally he experienced panic attacks, jolts of isolation, at the mention of Bi-Bo itself.

Meanwhile, he kept chiseling on his wood panels. In 2000, he even put his house on a neighborhood tour, until curiosity seekers poked their heads into the garage.

The more he learned about his wife's job, the deeper his rage. Using logomantic theories to arrive at the perfect five-letter name, he hired a detective named Frank Bogel to collect more dirt on Bi-Bo. Once again, Bi-Bo did not risk firing Athalie.

But they (their team) could easily threaten Leo. They leaned hard on me to stop Flucks, but to be careful with his wife. I didn't answer until my grant was not renewed.

A week later, the president of Bi-Bo ordered me into his office. The more ruthless his plan, the more even his smile. Please do not make me elaborate further. Since that meeting, I need antidepressants just to get to Friday. One more ounce of bad news, one more drop of spite, and I will fly like a pigeon and shit on your roof. Do not rub me the wrong way this month.

And yet, I was always the calm one. Look at my hands. They are twitching again. Nothing is physically wrong with me, just a fierce desire to strangle someone. I suddenly have exotic allergies I never heard of, unusual rashes that I picked up from my meeting at Bi-Bo.

After months of this oppressive scandal, I hatched a plan. No point wasting your time with it. Even I laugh. Make up your own ridiculous plot point here, anything that brings me to Flucks' house. I went there to force him to agree. But once I met him in his element, everything changed.

I arrived in unusually good spirits though. The birds were

mating and howling around his garage. I heard rather large animals scratching up in the date palms. The overgrowth resembled a lost island in a Jules Verne novel.

No one stopped me as I opened the garage door. The interior, at first glance, looked at least thirty feet squared, with shadows and highlights from a spiraling staircase below. It was a shed with a massive strutted glass ceiling, like a cross between a botanical hothouse and movie sets from the silent era. It also resembled an insurance office from late Victorian England. Rare woods dominated every corner. I couldn't read any of the carvings at first. The wainscoting combined every Louis style from 1620 to 1793, even with stamped leather and rocaille here and there. But then suddenly, it wasn't French at all. There were at least ten squares with words carved into the panels, each slightly larger than an old folio. They were inscribed with emblems you see on the frontispiece of Baroque books. I also noticed carved *hieroglyphica* (heretical copies of Horus Apollo or Horapollo) in a mishmash, along with Christian cabala, gnostic, even Jesuitical symbols. Flucks must have gathered these, or conjured them, from those crazy Roseauistes. Carved animals and archangels gleamed behind an odd paraffin varnish everywhere.

The smell was aromatic, as if sage, Artemisia and salvia plants were growing in hidden corners of the room, in pots somewhere, or through a ventilation shaft. I thought I heard something very big waking up, like a slow-moving whale squeezing the shed from outside.

The light didn't help clarify either. It was more a nest of spotlights, and fill lighting, mostly over the wooden sculpture nailed to the paneling, sometimes just with roofing nails. Scrawled above these was something like crude architectural models, like buildings. They clearly resembled Baroque streets, as well as lagoons, canals.

I wish I could say that some of this was brilliantly handled. But mostly, it looked very primitive, as if it had been carved during an invasion by mental patients. A few pieces had been bought; they were old, had some flourish. One chapel, or whatever it was, a shrine I guess, was filled with Oaxacan wooden animals, from Mexican villages. Each animal had been carved from a single piece of wood by a Oaxacan villager; no matter how twisted the branch, then painted in sunburnt oranges, peacock greens and mustard yellow. That made for a bright spot, like a clerestory.

All in all, it was suffocating, maddening and homely. But suddenly, I realized that I had been standing there looking for almost ten minutes. Feeling wobbly, I searched for a chair, while Flucks greeted me from thirty feet below. His voice seemed to hover along the walls. He climbed the spiral as he waved. Finally, I had my first clear look. He seemed much too normal, a straight nose, good cheekbones, like an aging, puffy Kafka, just another pale, frantic scholar unable to finish that object, unable to reproduce his profession.

But he was much more likable, exuberant, even gentle than I expected. I could see how weak he was. Even the stairs had exhausted him. He needed to sit on a mottled green couch. I found a shaky Indonesian stool nearby.

"May I begin our friendship by apologizing to you. Pretend I never said all that. I rarely mean exactly what I say. It's a problem I've had since my childhood. The point is now we have a common enemy. That should be our goal."

I tried to get past the amenities to explain that we had a common enemy, and test out my scheme. But he seemed not to listen, just humored me with a faint smile, began a story instead.

"Everything I tell you over the next hour will be a lie," he said. "Of course, that wouldn't really be a lie, would it? That would be more like a fact. The only way to really lie is by unreliably mixing it with the truth.

"Like you, I have been seriously considering strangling someone. But like you, I never get the right kind of encouragement. We can definitely help each other."

Then he gave me a tour. Five miniature cities coexisted for him in the same condensed space. He had blended these mostly from twenty copies of Venice. For him, false cities were like my research.

"I started with early Coney Island at first," He explained, "especially Freud's visit. The midgets and freak shows along Surf Avenue and on the Bowery fascinated me. In the distance, I saw false minarets. I tried to build cities on fire like those in Coney Island. There were also three versions of hell in the amusement parks there. And two ways to visit Creation. I particularly enjoyed going to the afterlife.

"Then I compared these to Disneyland in the year after it opened, when there were still a few carny barkers around, and donkey rides, a few traces of the old nickel empire, as Coney Island was called. But most of all, I was fascinated by the photos of those orange groves before they were cut down to make Disneyland, as if the smell of decayed oranges were still in the air.

"Finally, I considered Luxor in Las Vegas. Here was the first pyramid in 2,600 years, clearly an artifice. Klein says that one of the walls was made of styrofoam. The Flatiron Building sat directly above the Egyptian underworld.

"I expanded my research to any city where life and death coexisted as a themed space, as entertainment. Then I began putting together the project you see here. Along the way, I learned about the Roseau group, and their theories on false memory. Did you know that Freud's *Ephemera* mentions them as well? You should have read it carefully before you gave it up.

"What you see is my answer to the puzzle of imperfection. You'll notice that there is no entryway, no beginning. This took a lot of engineering, tricks with light."

Then he walked me down the spiral. Echoes literally circled us, like drafty weather. Each time they found us, he grabbed my hand, to keep from jumping out of his skin. Then he would start again.

"Around you is the product of ten years of sleepless enthusiasm. See the mix of styles? They are all a journey without a beginning. The sunlight is artificial–but no false dawn, no dusk, no movie tricks. Over there are ghostly mixes of false Venices in Vienna, Los Angeles, Las Vegas, Disney Epcot, even Dubai.

They all point toward the future that was promised, but never delivered. Many of the carved doors are just trompe l'oeil. Better to leave imaginary doors, as a fantasy about free will. Of course, I'm filled with bloated theories, like you, theories but no action.

"Anyway, what got me started were the false Venices. I found at least thirty. First I went to Vienna's Venice, at the Prater. It was built two years after Venice in Chicago (1893). Then three more Venices opened, one in Coney Island, another in St. Louis. The archives mostly confused me though. In 1904, the grandest Venice of them all began (at least until the Venetian in Las Vegas)—the town of Venice in southern California. Thousands of bungalows were placed near dozens of canals. Massive lagoons faced three piers filled with amusements, even a full-blown Piazza San Marco.

"Of course, no Venice equaled the first. None was completed without confusion. They were all maidens paying their regrets, to coin a phrase from Wordsworth. In Venice, California, first the drainage failed. Gondoliers in sombreros were suddenly covered with mosquitoes. In the twenties, cement buried most of the canals and the lagoons. Thus I found another somber shrunken Venice. In the thirties, oil wells leeched the soil. In 1964, two-thirds of Venice, California was bulldozed on a whim.

"Through my research, I circled the globe looking for a way to capture what all this told me. I discovered that every coast has its Venice. St. Petersburg was the Venice of the North. London has its Little Venice. Dubai is the Venice of Arabia. In Florida, the town of Venice had a city-beautiful piazza stuck inside a giant orchard. The Ringling Brothers Circus used to winter there. Today, it is identified as two and a half hours from Venice at Epcot.

"In my mind's eye, as you can see, one Venice lines up next to the other, like shrunken heads. See the Pepper's Ghost engravings over there? In the nineteenth century, copies of Tiepolo and Canaletto's imaginary Venice polluted the art market. There's Thomas Mann as Gustav Ashenbach before he dies slowly in

Venice. I was particularly struck by Calvino's version: Marco Polo and Kubla Khan inventing invisible cities that all resemble Venice.

"That brought me closer to the bottom of all this. Using Roseau systems, I began sketching imaginary versions of cities as one large architectural allegory–a single spiraling basement as a Venetian masquerade about the erasure of cities by tourism. It came to me after I bought a flyer from 1850 advertising all of Venice in one room. Nearly 16,000 miniature buildings, all to scale, promising a sunny Italian afternoon for the London businessmen on a long lunch.

"No nostalgia was allowed. My first rule. This building would be a space reenacting how we collectively forget. After all, except for the Venetian in Vegas, every one of these false Venices is a shell of its former self today (sometimes an expensive shell, but not much more). Even the Martian Venice–those canals on Mars–never were canals at all.

"You can imagine, particularly after my daughter was born, how much the pressures of fatherhood interfered. After three night feedings, with my wife missing again, who knows where, I had strange dreams. I would wake up as if I had been at a conference with the dead. The sounds delivered advice, and not in whispers, but like cats breathing in my face. I now know what they were saying, what the Roseauistes, and even Freud in Coney Island saw. They were right. Noises gather in spaces.

"I did travel once, spent almost a month in never Venice itself. I know what people say, but to me, it already seemed like another copy. I collected photographs of one Venice after another. You see the holograms below the cross bar? They aren't holograms. They are membrane-like projections, a new form of bacteria that record the vibrations of light and sound. You can touch them. Like opalescent skin from ten cities, they each rub against the other. Like electric fish, but they are no more than light. Nothing is solid when you can industrialize desire, don't you think? I went to thirty Venices, but to no place at all. I thought it was a kind of space travel.

"But my wife knew better. She convinced me in slow doses that I was mentally disturbed. I used to believe her, tried a cocktail of medications–until I found out about her plans. You read about those plans in the newspapers. As you like to say, please, don't ask me to discuss it.

He looked up toward a little girl, and pointed. "My daughter. Little pitchers have big ears.

"Let's be frank. Sometimes I wonder if my brain is as smooth as an eggplant. I am a mole. I live half below the ground. My marriage is also underground. Anyway, the more it dissolved, the more time I poured into my Venices down here. One day, I panicked and found that I just couldn't leave. Her adventures, however cruel to me, became my only way to mentally take myself out of this building.

"That's when I started to jump centuries. You notice that my Coney Island is set in 1904, but looks more like 1960, as if the Coney Island amusement parks hadn't burned down. I imagined 1904 going unchecked, as a parallel world surviving alongside our own.

"I tried to imagine Las Vegas going unchecked, never imploding its casinos. Next to that, you see a condensed citywalk for Los Angeles without freeways in 2005. But my centerpiece is still those twelve Venices–running parallel to each other. They are like stations of the cross. Each Venice floats in an amniotic light. Each intersects somewhere. See how they grow into each other, like furniture thinking it is still a tree, and growing into the wooden joists of the building itself."

I may as well finish this. From here Flucks gets rather incoherent. He knew his wife was running those lavish, silly vacations that Bi-Bo set up. But the more his marriage slipped way, the more he lived inside that basement, with its spiraling copy of thirty Venices.

One day, he discovered that he couldn't leave that hyperbolized garage. He had become utterly agoraphobic, couldn't leave for five minutes. Then like a pale breeze, his wife might visit once a day. She would bring the little girl, Miranda, into the garage.

Everyone would talk. His wife would confess to him. He began to enjoy her stories, while his rage grew.

Then he began to hear advice from the walls. But it wasn't advice. It was something else.

"I had this problem," he explained. "It was sound. Perhaps you heard of the phonon, the sounds inside a molecule? Occasionally, phonons begin to speak to you. Not with words, but your mind fills in the blanks. They are a locust swarm, shards of the past."

Lunch was brought. We ate anxiously. I tried to show good manners. No point threatening. Then up on the balcony, I saw his little girl playing. How had I failed to see her before? There was no sign of his wife. Just as suddenly, he tilted his head. He looked just like a dog hearing a sound; his face literally fell.

Then, as if an engine had started, I heard precisely what he was hearing—phonons inside his "machine," as the Baroque masters used to call a theatrical illusion. Imaginary gears and cams began to moan. At first the moan sounded like a gigantic truck without brake pads, that hissed, almost sparked. Then, all at once, I could have sworn that it sounded like a chorus of women screaming for help. Every thirty seconds, the moaning changed its point of reference, from men grunting near the ceiling to animals grunting instead, even to huge bladders hissing, as if my mind couldn't decide how to fly away.

Here I have to break off. I'm a mess, sweating through my shirt. The rest of the file has corrupted. Perhaps you would like the story to end with a Romantic flourish, the building collapsing around him. Or perhaps with Borgesian irony, as the parallel Venices begin to vibrate infinitely. Or maybe a Philip K. Dick ending, where no one quite knows whether they are corpses or alive. I tried to imagine how best to say what actually happened, even to add some insights on how Disney World, Las Vegas, Citywalk and Dubai might exist in the same architectural envelope.

But you undoubtedly want to know how Flucks planned to take revenge. At first, he wanted me to use my physical strength and repressed anger to strike out at our common enemies.

But then, the next day, I arrived to discover that he had changed his mind (such as it was). Suddenly, he resented my being able to come and go. He wanted, above all, to leave his Venices, walk out. I noticed that his daughter was back again, oddly cheerful.

He became more desperate than before. It was getting worse with those sounds, that electrical storm of oscillating, heaving, creaking, whistling.

Finally, his daughter understood what he wanted. She was only ten, but a stranger ten year old one cannot imagine, as if she were herself the container for thirty imaginary cities.

The little girl said: "We shouldn't play this way anymore, Bert (she called him Bert, like her mother). Should I stop?"

Then she simply climbed down to the main floor, kissed her father on the cheek, and drifted more than walked out, as if she were on a ship.

I listened as she went. Immediately all the strange noises ceased. It was utterly quiet, except for a modest wind on the glass roof, as if to say that it was signing off, heading north.

In the silence, Flucks put his hand on his head, and fell back. He lay there, perhaps from a stroke, occasionally quivering, as if from the cold.

I picked him up. Clearly that was, in the end, my job–to drive him to hospital, where they forwarded him like unanswered mail, to somewhere else for treatment.

I understand that he is partially cured, and suddenly struck with an odd loneliness. He talks obsessively to anyone who will listen, has become a remarkably funny raconteur, never the same facts twice. Someone should film him before this passes.

As for his wife, Athalie and I met last week. I have to say, I can understand why he held on to her. But her eyes seem to be shrinking with pain from the struggle. I think I can help her. So we'll be meeting tomorrow, nothing complicated, just lunch, to start.

I've also reentered Flucks garage. It has a lot of open space.

Perhaps I should bring some of my research on to the balcony. I can do some good work there, I think.

Here is the final problem in a nutshell: This book is a journey "between" worlds. To honor my subject, the last chapter has to never begin or end. But how does going in circles finish anything, structurally speaking? The clues have to add up. Even furniture piled in an attic makes a picture.

So I bring Leo back, for continuity. He looks newly minted–blinded with ecstasy. He is in the early stages of yet another great blunder. It will probably absorb the next ten years.

Leo recommends a short essay by Borges, entitled "Circular Time." Written in 1941, it reflects the grimmest point of World War II, the farthest advance by the Nazis. On the last page, Borges sketches out a brief parable, but never finishes it. He feels that *Léon Bloy* "should" have written the entire story instead:

"A theologian dedicates his entire life to refuting a heresiarch–a leader among heretics. First, he defeats his rival with intricate arguments. Then he denounces him, has him burned at the stake. Finally, in Heaven he discovers that in God's eyes, he and the heresiarch form the same person."

I can see why Borges imagined this for *Leon Bloy* (1846–1917). Here indeed was a forlorn heresiarch, a divided soul. In one breath, he condemned the modern papacy. With another, he was a Jewish converso to Catholicism. His spiritualism was thorny, literally about his suffering in this world; but also fiercely sexual and egoistical.

Borges felt that that Bloy prefigured Kafka. And Kafka compared Bloy to a harassed prophet in ancient Israel. Bloy's wide range of novels and political critiques (particularly a book defending the Jews in 1892) branded him an enemy of anti-Semitism, but also an anti-Semitic Jew–and finally a neo-cabalist and cryptographer, as in the following (his translation of a sentence by Saint Paul): "The pleasures of this world would be the torments in Hell, seen backward in a mirror."

Leo sees a parallel between his sex and Bloy (surely not Borges' sex life, gentle, retiring soul):

Bloy, in his youth, lived with a seamstress, essentially a loving *grisette*, who kept them from starving through prostitution. Then as a man in his thirties, he fell hard for a prostitute named Anne-Marie Roulé, but in Dostoyevskian fashion, eventually found her too holy for sex. Finally, while Bloy was away visiting a monk–who unfortunately, agreed with him–Anne-Marie took matters into her own hands. She sold her hair to a barber, who left her bald. With the money, she paid a dentist to have her teeth pulled out. Then for years, she and Bloy lived together as brother and sister, while he kept changing his mind, torn between regret and revelation.

So with Bloy in mind, if you bump into Leo hungrily pawing Flucks' wife, try to be understanding. Clearly, he's found a new way to lose himself, a new space between. And probably a new sentence to carve on his wall. The most repeated sentence by Bloy is:

"Man has places in his heart which do not yet exist, and into them suffering enters, to give them existence."

Overall, Leo should have stayed with that librarian from UC Riverside Special Collections. But who am I to say? I am absolutely not an expert on how to be happy.

I am more an expert on collective forgetting, though I pray for a rude awakening here. That may have finally happened. Two months ago, Hurricane Katrina startled millions of Americans. For three days, the Bush image machine lost control of the message. Over dinner, American viewers saw American corpses floating across an abandoned American city. The shock has dominated our politics ever since, and severely damaged Bush. Horrors in Baghdad conflated with horrors inside the Super Dome.

But we should not assume that every blink is a revolution. We must be prepared for a rough century. Even the fool's errand that we call the Bush presidency probably has a lot more disaster ahead. At least, the aftershocks will keep us hopping in all directions for decades.

However, for a month now, media pundits have been talking about the end of Bushismo, as if a new mini-era were arriving. Once again, the right-wing crusade that remade American politics after 1980 is failing, but probably not yet overturned. After all, the powers that sponsored it are as strong as ever—a combine of trans-national capitalists and energy brokers, in collusion with global media; and organized on the ground by fundamentalist Christians; while advised by conservative think tanks. Add to this a crucial fact, their ace in the hole, that population shifts help guarantee Republican domination of our politics—unless the old Confederacy breaks ranks, and a few of those red states join the Democratic column.

The broader problems will still remain, a political version of mass medication. For example, when media imagery takes hold, the truth or falsity of its "message" barely enters. Most of all, the strength of its impact counts. Americans generally assume that news is faked anyway. So instead of radicalizing our politics, dirty tricks simply erase the moral compass. Lies and facts become equivalent fictions, nothing more.

This erasure is comforting, a neutralizer. Even fifty years ago, C. Wright Mills already complained of "a creeping indifference and a silent hollowing out." Citizens are converted into an audience. Political images become as theatricalized as the interior of a Baroque church, or a special-effects movie. Special effects about losing your identity dominate the setting. It is an antechamber to a hundred staged entryways. Inside this playful space, life and death—war and crime—are choreographed as fictions.

Of course, to be so neutralized by special effects is an old and glorious tradition. Baroque illusion has simply been updated by the entertainment economy.

It is also a primal space, a theatricalized death watch. Thus, dreamwork is an antechamber; it neutralizes facts into fictions, to keep us sleeping.

Any medium that hypnotizes the audience relies on antechamber effects, from Greek tragedy to shopping malls. That includes computer spaces, hyper-links, computer games, scripted spaces at casinos. Slick Computer design tends to very slick; it converts any bottom line into an antechamber–any sugar coating applied to any surface. The list could go on for pages. None of us are immune to these effects, unless a Katrina-like trauma breaks the spell, rewrites how collective mental pictures are made–for a while.

Religion may be the ultimate antechamber, operatic in its organization of death and ritual. For me, it was an ending that never began.

As a teenager, I remember my father and his pals "dovening" (praying) at the synagogue. It was like sitting inside a Breughel painting. Dad always let me know that God was not under discussion, because the synagogue was just a neighborhood. The rabbi took care of God. The Torah took care of Avenue U and the butcher shop, particularly how to stay clear of gentiles. As for what to do in "shule" (synagogue), do not fall asleep. But if you do, know that God understands the pain of an ordinary man. That's the main thing, God has a simple heart.

I would pretend to mumble Hebrew fast, but mostly reread Ecclesiastes over and over in English, or the Song of Solomon (existential Torah and gorgeously pornographic Torah), while the buzz of inscrutable Hebrew songs ran through the little synagogue.

We were often between life and death, according to the prayers. But God was the soul of the earth. He knew hearts tended to stray. So this was surely the antechamber, a neighborhood between the unknowable and closing time.

On Yom Kippur, of course, the stakes ran higher. I was told not to have too much fun. With that in mind, and feeling sweaty, then feeling parched from the fasting, I stood for hours, peeking at the clock.

But even on the high holy days, while the cantor begged God to spare our lives for one more year, I heard bad jokes, and off-color stories about the local businesses, about childhoods in one European war or another, even about women's *poulkas* (thighs).

And I witnessed strange highlights, interludes.

One Yom Kippur, the village idiot came to pray. He could have been dropping in from the sixteenth century. He was a gentle retarded man, almost no chin, a receding forehead, and never quite shaven. On the street, you would see him tolerated like the town fool in old schtetels, or like the village idiots described by Foucault. Each store owner gave him a little to help out.

Outside, he always kept a cheap transistor radio to one ear. And when he saw me, aged fourteen, he always had the same question: "You have a wife? I'll marry her."

But today he entered the inner sanctum, where God smiled on lonely men. So he came without his radio, and wore something like a sports jacket. Looking anxious at first, he finally walked to where the prayer shawls were piled over a pew. He tried one on. Somehow, in his mind's eye, the shawl didn't fit. It felt too snug. So he dropped it to the ground. Then he tried on another. Too full in the shoulders. Again he tossed the holy-of-holy fringes on to the floor.

At last, the neighborhood had given him some freedom to choose, to be inside the embrace of the public. But meanwhile, the president of the congregation, a tall Polish hardware owner, was half-watching, half-rocking to each "Or-Main" (amen). Finally, this president just snapped, as if someone were running off with a set of wrenches.

At the precise moment when the cantor let God know that we live in charity, that our hearts were rich with good deeds, I heard a fight, a roar of voices. Everyone turned. The president had smacked this poor soul fiercely on the face.

"You throw the talis on the floor?" he threatened him "What are you crazy?"

God smiled as only He can. They were at it again. Which reminds me of another incident–the great struggle over curtains. It was a very humid Yom Kippur. Another president of the congregation, a short, round lozenge of a man, always in a blue suit, refused to let the women in the back rows keep the windows open. Again, the cantor's deep voice rose plaintively. This time,

I heard old women say: "You old bastard, we're dying of the heat back here." But he screamed back as good as he got.

This was not a world of tolerance. It was a place between–not Europe, not hallowed, not a work place, but not to be taken lightly, and yet an ironic place, where anything you said might be forgiven (but never tolerated). Once I tried to impress a girl by tossing my prayer book deftly on to a table. The rabbi smacked me in the face with another prayer book, then forgave me.

In our world today, these antechamber experiences are coveted again. We are in an age fraught with religious revivalism. The house of God provides a theater where momentarily the parishioner is not so much in a holy state, as inside a collective, ludic thrill. This can be both contemplative and profoundly theatrical–gauche, fierce, politically rigged–but as neighborhood, often very honest, whatever the beliefs may or may not be.

However, my medieval synagogue embarrassments so traumatized me, I still cannot formally join any organized movement, religious or secular, not even a yoga class. So I will never claim any moral high ground about my life as a citizen, not even over this reactionary, tinpot, Bushist mafioso combine. That would be an evasion. Everyone is caught in the same tragi-comedy, a space between worlds, inside a much larger drama: in this century, eco-threats of almost cosmic proportion.

We need a new political Enlightenment, a new social contract for nations, for global politics. I wish I had even a thousandth of what is required, simply to humanize the alienation properly.

Instead, I write about a space between, with an historian's look of astonishment. After all, the Enlightenment was not an age of reason; it was an age of dying political stupidities. The Renaissance was a miserable time to live, except for the courtiers lucky enough to kiss the ass of a prince–and for the well-born ass itself. As political bad faith, the space between helps every generation forget its stupid moments (but imagine that "we know how to remember"). The mental picture of whose ass got more than it deserved is often deleted like an expletive–modernity as slapstick–to cover up the embarrassments that came before, and the madness to follow. That way, it sort of never happened (for example, what may become of Bush), thus can definitely happen again.

First Conclusion: Freud Inside the Dragon

In 1909, Freud did indeed visit Coney Island. We know very little of what took place that day, nor during his week in New York, except that he and Jung also ate in Chinatown; then suffered from diarrhea. Apparently, many Europeans caught a bug of some kind in New York.

No fiction could be blunter than this, though Freud does pay a compliment once to the amusement parks in Coney Island. I ignored that fact. Fiction helped me talk more about mass entertainment. I could announce my artifices, like a ride in Coney Island. The "space between" could be widened.

Besides, it is near-impossible to objectively research a collective state of mind. For example, there is little evidence telling us whether Freud sensed World War I coming as early as 1909. However, I have researched thousands of sources on how World War I was imagined before it took place. From 1871 on, in many forms of the popular press, there was an incipient sense of a darkness coming. This literature (particularly books about tank warfare, and aerial bombardment) accelerated after 1910. It was clearly woven into English and French science-fiction literature and futuristic illustration.

So it is tempting is to imagine the state of mind in Europe as hovering on the brink of military suicide. This assumption, essentially a fiction, seems to explain the facts. The Balkan wars had already begun. The militarism, the war industries, and racist madness were already in place. The mood of nightmare-to-come floats in modernist avant-gardes, from 1909 to 1913, particularly in the bombast of Futurist manifestoes, in the clippings about war put in the corners of Cubist collages, in the prophetic writing of young critics, like Appolinaire and Charles Péguy, who both died during the First World War.

With all this evidence of fantasy warfare piled throughout my house, I try to fictionalize what amusements in Coney Island Freud might have fancied. Very likely, in my fictional mind's eye, he was appalled (morally, ideologically). Certainly, he was appalled by America.

In Coney Island, he could not have avoided Dreamland. At its entrance, Dreamland featured what Disney later would call a Big Wow—a thirty foot naked woman in plaster, known as Creation. In order to pass the gate, Freud would have essentially walked under her looming vagina, then navigated into one pre-conscious attraction after another, from freaks to dwarfs to Hell.

Four years later, Freud complained about patients who dreamt in mass-culture imagery, whose dream work restaged imagery from popular wood engravings by Gustave Doré. Then Freud left blanks in the record. Those blanks are extremely powerful signals. By 1909, the entertainment economy was not yet industrial strength (Freud saw his first moving picture on the day after his visit to Coney Island).

Nevertheless, we know very little about what Freud thought was the impact of mass culture upon the psyche, even in the thirty years after 1909. He wrote about folklore invading the collective process, about war trauma, about the ghoulish entrapment by machines, about Leonardo's latent homosexuality, but barely a word on the visual entertainments that proliferated around him (amusement parks, illustrated weeklies, cinema, department stores, signage on stores).

Today, of course, that has been utterly reversed. From the mid-fifties into the late eighties, postmodern theory was literally a total immersion into consumer entertainment (both critical and worshipful): how it warps our sign systems, generates perverse mythemes, distorts our memory, floods us with simulacra. Mass culture took on the hyperbole of a crime novel, where nothing can be trusted, a globalized antechamber about banalized deconstructions, floating signifiers, rhizomatic drift, epistemic contagion.

Of course, postmodernism ended in the early 1990's, for the most part. There is not even a name for our era (I like to call it the Electronic Baroque, even electronic feudalism). But one fact is dead certain: terms like consumerism and mass culture seem naive now. Today we all live essentially inside the stomach of the "entertainment" dragon: yet another model for antechambers. Trans-national effects (from media to architecture and politics) make it nearly impossible to generate an avant-garde–or even a postmodern–strategy. Not in a world where shopping malls are doubling as streets, where cities are being rescripted into antechambers. Try to find a major boulevard anywhere in Europe or the United States that hasn't been retooled into a kind of outdoor mall.

As a hundred major critics have already explained: entertainment design has recoded not just architecture, but also the fine arts, publishing, probably sexual foreplay. It also supports ruthless policies, for a renewed capitalism based on simulation. This simulation has passed beyond theories about semiotic drift. It has matured into a structured power grid. It systematically withers away the middle class as easily as the working poor. It promises to violate the so-called American dream, help us laugh our way toward bankruptcy. It has a whimsical way of being dead serious.

Thus, the dragon is not merely entertainment. It is any industry that relies on media effects, branding campaigns, glossitecture and architainment. Nor is it simply fascist, like Europe between 1922 and 1945. We have to relax our hyperboles, and avoid as many twentieth century parallels as possible.

Obviously, these effects are the most sophisticated antechambers of our time. Their techniques are very shrewd. They are often very bawdy and unsentimental, comic like a Breughel painting, or a Jan Stein painting, or a taste of Swift, Bierce, the acid dripping from page to page.

Special effects translate these metaphors into objects as solid as a crowbar, very much in the spirit of Swift or Phillip K. Dick. Antechambers become sci-fi hardware. They are machines that collectively harvest a sci-fi forgetting in the future. At the movies, we visit a city after the apocalypse, like dropping in at own funeral. Then we try the new Italian restaurant next door. By pretending to make it glamorously awful, special effects teach audiences to love surveillance, to not require much public or intimate life. They show the public how to enjoy the wait, neither inside nor outside, to hover between doorways. Be an audience wherever you go. Better still, buy a copy of the game, be a player. But never attack the program, only pretend that you are a warrior.

"Turn" is the appropriate verb here. When politics merges with special-effects antechambers, it turns the fictional side of photographs into political advertising. It helps convert elections into shopping. Also, special-effects architecture remodels streets for tourism. That helps turn us into tourists in our own cities; and then in our own bodies.

Second Conclusion: The Cipher

But as literature, this matter of "space between" is quite a different matter, a deep contrast to politics. There are many effective (and I believe, gently intimate) ways to build literature about antechambers. They go back to the dawn of print, to "the birth of tragedy." I still plan another volume where I review gothic special effects from revenge dramas in seventeenth century England to condo lofts in downtown suburbia today–gothic revival noir, cyber slapstick goth architainment, post-neo-retro...

But for now, let us narrow to the form we see in front of us, to the page. An antechamber can easily be turned into a poem or a play–into grains of text. Here we find an ancient poetics of resistance, dating back to the Greeks. It has often been said that absence is presence in literature. Blanks, elisions, excisions speak loudly, because they are silent. We can find this in the way poetry is edited down (line breaks, grammatical fractures). Also in how paragraphs are edited in a novel, like jump cuts–how point of view shifts from one character to another, through excisions, and sudden shifts in tone.

And we can micro-edit even further, to clauses, and to short forms only paragraphs long, but made for absence—like the aphorism. These become building blocks for new work, that can enrich photography, film, even politics, advertising, and certainly the digital arts.

As story, absences reveal how people forget, how fictions complete facts. Imagine a blank no wider than a hair. But still you sense it. What you sense is more than deconstruction, more than a clue in a detective story. It is a keyhole; it leaves room for your mind's eye to work. That is, for layers of memory to "drop a stitch," mash an image.

Every literary medium uses absence as the key to its power. The novel is blind. Thus, its visual imagery is overwhelming. For example: "As she lie there, her blood was a color that he couldn't quite fathom." Try to shoot that in a movie. Very tough. But as blind text, it is easy.

Similarly, narrative film is autistic. So its film grammar (camera angles, lighting, editing) exaggerates point of view. The passionless camera leaves blanks to take you inside the mind of characters. Provocative blanks. Indeed, the senses that are missing help a medium speak.

In 2002, I was asked to apply these theories to a novel about absence and forgetting (and LA history). The novel was inserted inside a DVD-ROM. I finally had my own train set to play with.

I'll review briefly what I discovered: The project orbited around a story about an old woman named Molly who we meet in 1986. Molly has systematically "forgotten" a murder that she may have committed twenty-seven years before. Inside her mental neutrality—her "antechamber"—she refused to perform like a character in fiction. She would not act out the part of the suffering noir "bitch" anti-heroine. She also ignored all the best noir clues. She lived near dozens of famous film-noir locations, where movie murders were committed near her house, and her place of business (downtown); but never saw the films, preferred comedies instead.

With the team at Labyrinth (Rosemary Comella at USC), and with Andreas Kratky (then at ZKM), we filtered through thousands of photographs, hundreds of thousands of newspaper clippings, and hundreds of films in the USC archive. For the viewer, these were supposed to generate story through what was left absent, unsaid. They encourage the viewer to mentally fill in the blanks—the missing plot points—to make absences present.

As an engine for this "interactive" pleasure, the "assets"—photo, films and video—streamed in three layers, with blanks strategically scripted inside. Layering became the discipline for every element, inside the interface, the streaming of the visuals. That meant layers of Los Angeles, layers in Molly's memory; and forgetting, in the way photography manipulates the facts. Or how cinema distracts us. These palimpsests "covered" sixty years.

We compared literary absence to the camera lens. I called these mental ellipses "apertures"—erasures—with Baudelaire as my model. Baudelairian correspondence allows images to never illustrate, to never quite match their captions, thus leave absences. Photos reveal gaps within text and the city itself. Thus, photography cannot be anything but fictional. It camouflages while it reveals—particularly in the movies, but also in the common photograph. Photography becomes streaming points of view, a collective stream of consciousness, in echoes, homages to Joyce, Woolf, Lawrence Sterne, Musil, etc.

Third Conclusion: Possums and Monkeys

With my hands still awkward with this silly arthritis, I rummage through my archive room after the rainy season, wondering if the back room is slipping down my hilly backyard, like a boat barely tethered to the dock. I fill a crate with references to "absence" from some of my literary heroes.

In the short story, "An Unwritten Novel," Virginia Woolf uses absence as a furtive trick, a glimpse by the writer: "Whether you did, or what you did, I don't mind; it not the thing I want. The draper's window looped with violet—that'll do; a little cheap perhaps, a little commonplace–since one has a choice of crimes, but then so many (let me peep across again–still sleeping, or pretending to sleep)."

In the opening to *Mademoiselle de Maupin* (1837), Théophile Gautier describes the absence between "circumstance" and desire: "This life, although I have in appearance accepted it, is scarcely made for me, or at least is very far from resembling the existence of which I dream, and feel myself designed."

I gather phrases, like "the waves of lucidity... made scarce by the rain," in Marquez's *Hundred Years of Solitude*; or the ripeness of life moments from decay (as in the French for still life, *mort vivant*) in Proust's descriptions of art and fragrance in *The Guermantes Way*. Or Louis Aragon's surrealist vision of shops and workers at the arcades in Paris (*Paris Peasant*, 1926). Or Laurence Sterne attempting to make a straight line that maps his Uncle Toby's stories. Or Poe designing another literary hoax.

In historical writing, absence is the space between a fact and a collective guess, whether by the historian (who turns the dots into a line), or by a moment as you live it, often so tough to historicize until years later. In architecture, absence is something you see in fissures. It is the space where unfinish is revealed, the *détournement*, essentially the fissure that reveals traces of old mistakes, half-completed projects, and erasures.

Daydreams are clearly antechambers of a kind. Let me try daydreaming, see what pops into my mind: The stiffness in my hand never quite normalizes. I daydream that at least I don't have an infected root canal. Talk about odious comparison. The nerves inside my root canal grew back, after they had been removed incompletely, then got re-infected.

I linger in cheerful morbidity for hours, daydream about taking revenge on evil bureaucracies. I imagine myself seventy-eight years old, finally noticed as a writer. I am on a panel at Harvard. The demonic moderator tries to erase my biography, wants me to bark for my lunch. But I am now a surgical debater. Like Holmes, I prove that he has been sexually abusing a graduate student. His wife is shocked. The audience sees that my political intentions are honorable. I have all the great lines.

The night still feels antibiotic. Susan Sontag had a great opening line for it: "Illness is the night-side of life, a more onerous citizenship." Then in her book (*Illness as Metaphor*), she explained that was not emigrating to this kingdom.

This little book does not travel there either, not really. It is more about being "in between," about the "dual citizenship (between) the well and the kingdom of the sick." In literature, this has always been a perversely theatrical place, as well as a very gothic one, as in my tales about death watch. I also use "the space between" as a prop to discuss the hollowing out of the American psyche, a metaphor that is neither fact nor fiction. My book is more about theatricalized diseases that exist immaculately, without bodily causes. The patient endures metaphorical (or should I say metonymic) symptoms, an ontological process inside a teleological mystery. That's different than Sontag.

... I just heard Leo at the door. When he walks in, my living room shrinks by half. Athalie, his new flame, doesn't quite look as I imagined her, not anymore. I listen for phonons making voices, but nothing comes out of the woodwork.

"My new research is aphorisms," Leo tells me. He goes on in bursts, like aphorisms, until finally I cannot make heads or tails out of much. All three of us pretend that he has learned a profound lesson of some kind.

But Leo has inspired a plan. I will complete the philosopher's circle–cross without a start or a finish. I will gather aphorisms from my archives, and deliver a few, as my last word on absence, antechambers, cities, and gothic theatricality, morbid pleasures, and ghosts. Then I'll wind it up with my best guess for the future of forgetting.

I think of aphorisms as fragrant in Henry James' sense. The fragrance drifts away just as we approach it, like the possum I see crossing the street. The possum sports that prehensile tail, like a pig-sized rat, or a hairless, bloated monkey.

Fourth Conclusion: The Hummingbird Effect

Then a hummingbird stops in front of my window. The wings resemble a ferocious little automaton. It is modernity incarnate, except for a fundamental problem. The hummingbird is not moving at all. It is so fast that it is standing still. That is our new panoramic modernity. We fly ahead at such intense speeds that in fact, we are standing still, like an email from Antarctica, like a movie trailer edited so fast, you no longer see any places within the story, just a blur of action. Its wings seem to agonize. Their stillness looks ragged, like white noise, or suds for washing clothes, a machine that runs fast enough to stay in place, not go forward nor backward really.

We fly to another continent, but find the same ten stores waiting there. Even eerier, the airport back home has been shipped to a foreign city. Maybe they have tanker jets that can do that. What's more, this airport was restocked en route. Now it sells foreign snacks, and foreign newspapers. Otherwise, it feels almost the same.

Air travel relies on the hummingbird effect, as does the Internet; and all telematic media, all multiple-user computer games. For years, technophiles said that speed meant unvarnished progress, more of the wonder of endless circulation. Now we know better, at the least about the tradeoffs. Along with shipping the airport from one continent to another, globalization brought ten thousand new varieties of repetition, more games about infinite choice in a world of absolute predestination. Hummingbird is another metaphor for our globalized, low-grade nervous breakdown, to go like a hummingbird with user-friendly software stored inside our skull.

And today, we even have a war that may turn into a thirty-year hummingbird effect. And the providers of speed have designed excuses for poverty so intense that the gulf between rich and poor now rivals what existed in the fifteenth century. Of course, we still have new toys coming. They say that improved cell phones may one day perform minor surgery, or talk to the dead (the theoretical dead, kept in files, but still waiting for our call).

Years ago, I imagined billboards for outer space. That way, people stuck for years inside space stations could have something to see out the window that made them feel more at home. They could pretend that their space station was a truck barreling down a mountain road, past billboards, while hauling cross country.

The Morph Versus the Collage

The morph freezes instantaneous time. Each instantaneity is stacked in layers. Each layer hides one another. Thus, as in an airport, you never leave, you only arrive. Only the newspapers are not the same at the newsstand.

That is what we offer at Morphon Townhouses. Just imagine how many layers we can stack inside each bedroom. The bathrooms literally take you through every part of your body. And when it's time for bed, our machines gently rinse your vital organs for the night, without your knowing it. The suturing follows an eccentric loop while you sleep. At last, three rooms that are very diffuse, yet highly centralized.

There

The sheer madness of our future is that Americans have already gotten there, and didn't feel terribly different. As a basic principle of ergonomics, (1989–2001), consumer marketing cushioned us against future shocks. The twentieth century was noisier. It was massified and loud, with grinding steel monsters, glass curtain walls, carpet bombing, sixteen-wheelers, lawn blowers and sirens.

But this century is nannofied. Accessories grow smaller with each season. The future is small enough to wear, as our body steadily neutralizes. We barely hear ourselves crashing.

Noise is out. It ruins photos and data, but never our concentration (remember white noise?). We buy noise reduction for airplanes, cars, media systems. We insulate against passive and active frequencies, to hollow out noisy interiors. We protect against surges from electricity–as well as surges in fluid transfer during sex.

But what troubles me is that I am obsessed about quiet also. I carry foam air plugs in little vials. In 1900, that was a symptom of nervous collapse. Now it means that you buy smart media and have good surfaces. But that wouldn't be me. So I must be a Victorian neurasthenic.

A few sentences on the *hollowing out* of America: As of 1950, it often implied something "mental," an unconscious Freudian displacement, or a sociopathic inwardness. Similarly, vampires hollow out their victims. The philosopher hollows out a place in the mind. Industrial culture hollows out the social (Simmel, Adorno, Habermas). The outdoorsman hollows out a canoe.

By 1985, it suggested the end of democratic decision making, and thereafter, a tracking device for understanding each stage of globalization (the shrinking of national governance).

For Deleuze and Guattari, hollowing out entailed a monumental *tombeau de devenant*, the art of being eternally embalmed. I see hollowing out as the psychological cost of horizontalized power.

Living Sideways and Horizontally

Our culture is certainly more horizontal than vertical–outsourced, globalized, multi-tasked, acentered. And yet highly centralized, often like a beached whale, massive but immobile, unable to start from scratch, or engage the present structurally, with new forms. Only technology, the gadgetry of our culture easily changes shape–shape shifts–almost every year. The novel, the movie, the video game, theater, TV, museum crating, and dozens of other cultural forms might as well be carved on stone and left to weather on Mount Sinai. The eleventh commandment for culture is "thou salt polish, but never break."

Too much polish freezes the dynamic of story. It turns even

the present into nostalgia; and the future into a past tense. Careers in the arts and media become much trickier to navigate, because there is practically no visibility except at the top. The experimental arts are even more ignored by gargantuan distribution mafias that cannot bend far enough to drink through a straw; and continually defend their lethargy and reactionary planning as good business. In fact, they suicidal reduce business.

Emotionally, this hollowing out is our mode of alienation, more like a cyber than a Jekyll and Hyde–hollow and invaded, not impacted and ingrown. (I obviously have labored over that point.) We feel plundered by the entertainment economy. Emotional pain is catheter with great difficulty.

In place of old Freudian models (as dozens of theorists have shown), privacy becomes a defense against intimacy. We clearly worry about identity theft, but welcome surveillance. It is a sociable way to enjoy media.

A Final Architectural Metaphor: The Antechamber in Los Angeles

For decades in Los Angeles, the Belmont Tunnel served as portal to the underworld–for Graff art, pre-Columbian ball games and alien invasions. It was probably the largest urban ruin in the United States, over a mile long. The Pacific Electric trolley company completed it in 1925, as the westerly mouth of the tiny Hollywood Subway spur for the vast LA trolley system (1,100 miles long). The tunnel started downtown at 455 North Grand, emptied through the portal at Beverly, then fed northwest into Glendale, Burbank, Hollywood and the San Fernando Valley.

On the site, trains were stored and repaired at the Toucan Yard adjoining the tunnel, beside a tiny, moderne power station. However, even by 1925, the Yard was already a mess, fully saturated with runoff from oil derricks and creaky wooden wells; then later, with spills from a Shell Station in the forties.

The area symbolized industrial circulation. Trolleys snaked underneath the large First Street Bridge (1929) that overwhelmed the area from the South, like a giant El.

The only cultural feature that managed to survive was the Bob Barker Marionette Theater, still standing just north of the bridge.

Not surprisingly, around the tunnel, Beverly Boulevard ceased development, though houses on hillsides above it continued to be built. The noise and smoke undoubtedly rose straight into people's windows, but the thrum of interurban red cars could be soothing at night, like whales humming underwater.

The neighborhood started out, and remained relatively poor. When the tunnel was shut down in 1955, adjoining real estate was still identified as "working class." Bob Pimenko, a steel worker, bought the large craftsman house just above the tunnel in 1954, with his brother, who died fifteen years ago.

Bob still lives there, with a black woman who had been homeless, had lived near the tunnel. He remembers the forties most of all–jitterbugging to Louis Armstrong in dance halls a mile east, on Figueroa and Ninth. His black lady friend tells me that he can "still really dance." He has an amazing smile, like the coast of Scotland, every tooth a different length.

Bob never experienced many problems (not graffiti or crime). So he just settled in while Anglos steadily moved out after 1965, even after the general area was redlined by racist insurance companies. Then by the mid eighties, the abandoned tunnel area had been reclaimed by the largely Mexican community nearby, but as an antechamber between worlds, as if to honor the underground journeys it once delivered.

The empty tracks and yards, baked and brown like Mexico, were converted into something like a pre-Columbian ball field. Immigrants from Michoacan played a ball game there called Tarasca, directly descended from games older than the Conquest. Three men faced each other on each team, and the system for counting points was essentially the same as five hundred years ago. All they lacked were the embroidered gloves typical of Tarasca players in Michouacan.

According to myth, the ancient Mexican ball fields were portals—antechambers between opposing worlds, twin faces: life and death; upper and lower; human and divine; drought with fertility. Of course, the centuries of Spanish rule mostly erased these as active belief. But traces have a bizarre way of evolving. Games survived in Sinaloa, Michouacan, Guerero and Oaxaca, with different names in each region. Some rituals from the ball courts also survived in the cemeteries.

After 1983, far inside the mouth of the tunnel, and along 300 hundred feet of blank walls outside, graffiti artists started to operate: Risco City (the first major piece), Primo-Bee, Los Angeles Bomb Squad, NASA Crew, TWA, GEONE, Kill To Succeed, Second to None, MAK, L2S. The Belmont Tunnel quickly became the premier location for graffart in California, hosting crews from as far off as Chicago and New York. The neighborhood even sponsored cross-town competitions. The tunnel itself was featured in dozens of music videos, like Red Hot Chili Peppers' "Under The Bridge," and as the site for an AIDS benefit with Snoop Doggy Dog in 1999.

That year, I took UCLA graduate students there, with flashlights to help you not fall into the puddles in ruts along the old track, and strange pockets in the walls for workers to nestle while trolleys rattled by; all gone, but still present.

One impressionable architect claimed that his video camera recorded ghosts and mysterious sounds there, something gleaming off the moisture along the walls. In class, he excitedly installed his tape to show us; but it instantly erased itself, went blank.

Every few months, the city reattached new chain link fences around the Tunnel. But these were always torn open. Police occasionally studied the graffiti walls for clues to troublesome taggers, but did not roust the homeless who lived there, not even the feral dogs hiding behind wooden favelas inside the little station. There was an understanding, of sorts. Occasionally, city trucks would dredge up hundreds, even thousands of empty spray cans. Sometimes, health officers sprayed chemicals, a half-assed attempt at disinfection.

Dozens of photographers have recorded the tunnel, layer by layer. A German filmmaker scooped up various junk that he could find, and brought it back to Munich. Urban archaeologists studied the mouth of the portal itself. They found at least ten layers, like ten entries into Orc. The first read "To Oblivion," painted on the day the tunnel closed (June 15, 1955; the trolley cars were later sold in Latin America.) Afterward, among the tags: Red Car Tunnel, Des, CAR, CASH in 2000, then CAR again.

Since 2003, the tunnel has been endangered, and now is being destroyed. Meta Housing Corporation, who specialize in Neo-Tuscan Nevada-style apartment complexes downtown, has finally won the tug of war against neighborhood activists who wanted to save the tunnel. The walls are gone. The tunnel (already cut in half by the foundation fro the Bonaventure Hotel) is now only a façade, designated a historic monument.

As in other parts of the world, from Amsterdam to Beijing, only the shallow historical surface is maintained, while the historical memory around it—even inside and behind it—is distracted into tourist amnesia. In 2005, oil storage tanks were removed badly, and methane gas is still present underground. So there is some mitigation going on, slowing down development for a few more months. But the Northwest Gateway will go up, 276 units (20% low income), at a cost of nearly $60 million.

Los Angeles has a housing shortage, so that is the official argument on behalf of Northwest Gateway. Too often, that argument justifies bulldozers in poor neighborhoods. But warehousing people without a cityscape carefully in place has not worked before, and very likely will look like a space station caught in between, as it has hundreds of times elsewhere.

The future of forgetting is clearly upon us, as downtowns are turned into suburban bedroom communities, and horizontal trans-national capitalism sets the tone for our medicated civilization. Meanwhile, this week the riots in France continue for the tenth day, another forty people died in Iraq, weather shocks continue in the worst hurricane/tornado/tsunami season in over a hundred years.

The medication may not work much longer. But the anguish and silliness will undoubtedly be our quixotic gift to the future. We cannot polish away that much contradiction, even with the best special effects and hidden effects.

The Belmont Tunnel was also a special effect, premier location for movies about gothic sci fi and urban descents into the portals of hell. In the popular mini-series *V* (1983, with sequels afterward), Nazified aliens invade earth, and battle hunky young resistance fighters inside the tunnel. *Predator 2* docked its space cruiser there. Sadists visited in *Reservoir Dogs, Colors, Training Day*. Graffiti from the walls was regularly slipped in many other films. Dozens of documentaries and film collections survive of it.

The antechamber is finally a mental phantom made solid, like an animated world turned upside down–particularly for an economy where illusions psychologically invade, then are built, as if by a cock-eyed plastic surgeon. Finally, everything looks a bit fictionalized. That way, the bridge effect never begins or ends. As one tagger explained, the tunnel is "a place that no longer exists in the physical sense, but in the mind is infinite."